What she felt for him gripped her hard. Still, even after weeks together, she hardly knew him.

With his newfound ability to talk, she could now ask him the question that burned through her every time she felt the softer emotions swirl in her heart. She was afraid to hear his answer, for should it be affirmative she would be crushed. She could never love a man whose moral character she could not condone. She valued life too much.

The question begged to be asked. So simple to give voice and finally put to rest her own doubts. Simple, yes, but staring into his eyes, so hopeful and vulnerable, made her ashamed to believe the flapping tongue of Mrs. Burns over a man whose sincerity she had witnessed time and again. But she had to ask.

"There is a rumor," she said, her voice low and intense, "that you murdered someone."

His expression shifted ever so slightly. Surprise mingled with something else, and his gaze skittered to the surface of the table.

She closed her eyes and swallowed, recognizing what his averted gaze meant. Not the innocence she had hoped for, but resignation. Even fear.

S. DIONNE MOORE is a multi-published author who makes her home in Pennsylvania with her husband of twenty-one years and her daughter. You can visit her at www.sdionnemoore.com.

Books by S. Dionne Moore

HEARTSONG PRESENTS
HP912—Promise of Tomorrow

Promise of Yesterday

S. Dionne Moore

Heartsong Presents

For Lauren, the next writer in the family. You've overcome so much and still retain your sense of humor. It is hard to believe you are the same baby who struggled for life for seventy-five days, and I can only marvel at the young woman you are becoming. *Te quiero.*

A note from the Author:
I love to hear from my readers! You may correspond with me by writing:

S. Dionne Moore
Author Relations
PO Box 721
Uhrichsville, OH 44683

ISBN 978-1-61626-080-4

PROMISE OF YESTERDAY

All scripture quotations are taken from the King James Version of the Bible.

All of the characters and events in this book are fictitious. Any resemblance to actual persons, living or dead, or to actual events is purely coincidental.

Our mission is to publish and distribute inspirational products offering exceptional value and biblical encouragement to the masses.

PRINTED IN THE U.S.A.

one

Marylu Biloxi took careful aim with her broom. "You stagger yourself around somewhere else, Zedikiah. We don't take to your drunken binges, and you're a shame to the rest of our young black folk."

Zedikiah blinked hard in the waning sunlight. His dark skin and bloodshot eyes gave evidence of his hearty patronage of anyone who slipped him corn liquor.

Marylu swung the broom at the back of his baggy britches. "Now get. You near mowed down Miss Rosaleigh, and I'll not have you knocking over any more of Miss Jenny's customers."

Miss Jenny McGreary, owner of McGreary's Dress Shop, the best dress shop in Greencastle, Pennsylvania, appeared on the boardwalk beside Marylu. "Let him go. Miss Rosaleigh's fine. Besides, she's got her head so far into the clouds these days, *she* probably ran into *him*."

Marylu leaned on her broom and chuckled, the sun warm on her head. "You sure right about that. Never seen a woman so scatterbrained." Her mirth faded when she turned back to Zedikiah, who swayed on his feet. "His mama, the Lord rest her weary soul, would have his head in that trough for acting the way he does."

An idea popped into her head. Zedikiah stared at her with an unfocused gaze and slack jaw. Marylu crept closer and grabbed the back of his scrawny neck. His slight frame had no chance against her robust figure and greater weight as they took the steps down into the street. If not for her hand on his collar, he would have sprawled face-first into the mud. Marylu stopped him in front of the trough, bent him double, and dunked his head into the warm, horse-slobbered-in water.

"Marylu!" Miss Jenny's voice held horror.

"His mama would do the same. Since Dottie's not here to haunt him into sobriety, I'll take the job."

Miss Jenny pressed her lips together, her eyes on the trough. "Oh, dear. Marylu. . ."

Seeing her employer's concern, Marylu noted that bubbles were slower in getting to the surface. She pulled the boy upright and gave him a good shake to rattle his brain to wakefulness.

Zedikiah sucked in gulps of air, color flushing back into his cheeks. He started sputtering and spewing.

Marylu let him go, and he promptly slumped at her feet. But as he sat in the dust of the worn road, something tugged hard at her heart. He'd lost his mama near a year ago and him not even fourteen. "Time for you to stop your wild ways," she huffed and bent to help him to his feet.

"You go on over to my house." Jenny touched the boy's arm. "Cooper will get you some dry clothes and warm milk."

But Miss Jenny's words didn't seem to penetrate Zedikiah's stupor. When the boy swayed on his feet, Marylu caught hold of his arm, noticing, again, how large her hand appeared against his scrawny bicep. Drinking himself to death, he was. She would have to keep a closer eye on Zedikiah, else his wild ways were going to land him in a real stew.

Miss Jenny patted the boy's back and turned. "I have to get back to Miss Rosaleigh," she threw over her shoulder.

Marylu frowned at the boy and released his arm. "Zedikiah?" She waited for him to look at her, but his head remained sunk between his shoulders, eyes on the ground. "You do what Miss Jenny just said. Have Cooper get you something to eat." But her words still seemed not to penetrate the fog of the boy's drink-addled mind. With a heavy sigh, she left him in the street, turning back once to see him stumbling down the road. At least he was headed west, toward Miss Jenny's place. She hoped he had understood after all.

Inside the shop, Miss Rosaleigh Branson stood before

the dressmaker's model in the corner, inspecting her ivory wedding gown, not seeming the worse for wear from her brush with Zedikiah. Marylu shook her head at the sounds of the young white woman's sighs and giggles, as her hand brushed over every single detail of the gown.

"Let's get you into this," Jenny suggested as she motioned the bride-to-be to a smaller room out of sight of the front door.

Marylu dismissed Zedikiah's binges and the sad state of the thirteen-year-old boy's future and set about her chores. She ducked back outside to draw water to mop the floors, where mud from recent rains mottled the hardwood planks. Wouldn't do a fig to have Miss Jenny's floors so dirty. Not with all the highfalutin clients she served.

The motion of scrubbing the wood floors brought a song to her lips, and she sang low and mournful of a people in Bible days released from slavery of a different kind. She got to the second verse, when the two women emerged from the back room.

Miss Branson gravitated to the large mirror and gave a squeal of delight, punctuated by a little jig.

Marylu couldn't help but laugh.

"Careful there, Miss Branson. Those pins of Miss Jenny's will poke you full of holes."

"I'm getting married!" The young woman sighed as she brushed a hand down the spotless material.

"You sure are." Miss Jenny crossed the room and knelt beside the young bride-to-be. She folded the material at the hem and secured it with a pin. "You'll be a beautiful bride."

Marylu caught the wistfulness in her employer's tone and harrumphed. Jenny paused her pinning and the two exchanged a smile.

It was an old subject. One they had discussed and lamented many times. Marylu believed her employer should get married, to which Miss Jenny would turn the tables and try and convince Marylu to give marriage a chance.

Marylu's answer was the same then as it was now. "No one's going to see me popping over a man like grease in a hot skillet." With that, she leaned forward to resume scrubbing, her knees cracking in protest to the abuse.

As her employer finished up with Miss Rosaleigh, Marylu scrubbed with vigor at the dried mud. She should have done this yesterday when it seemed every dainty-booted foot crossing the threshold held some chunk of muck to be ground underfoot, but she'd been too busy hemming skirts. Now she paid for the neglect by having to scrape extra hard at the crusty filth. Her back ached as she worked the stiff bristled brush. She stopped long enough to allow Miss Rosaleigh to float past and make her exit, doubting the girl even felt the floor beneath her feet.

"You know, Miss Jenny," Marylu stoked the embers of the old argument, "that widower at the mill sure would be a good one for you. Don't you want to be floatin' around like the ones you stitch such fluff for?"

"Sally Worth has her eye on him already."

Marylu recognized the resigned tone. Jenny McGreary was a plain woman, and older than most of marrying age at twenty-five, while Sally was much younger and very pretty. Little by little, Marylu had seen Jenny's girlhood dreams of marriage and family wither.

Before she could gather her thoughts enough to say something comforting, the creak of the door's hinges signaled another customer. The prospect of dainty, dirty boots getting ready to smear her clean floor made Marylu huff and sit back on her heels. She'd make sure this patron wiped her feet. But the form that appeared inside the door was not of feminine persuasion, and the booted feet were neither dainty nor clean.

The black man raised his hat and grinned down at her. His grizzled black hair, touched with gray, seemed to explode from his head, and she wondered how he managed to keep a hat on at all with such a springy mop. It was when her eyes lighted on the thick mud crusting his boots that Marylu's normally stiff knees got some youthful spring back into them.

"Don't know what you're doing, but you're not crossing my floor with those muddy boots."

Miss Jenny headed their way, a dark frown, aimed at discouraging Marylu's tongue, marring her features. Marylu knew if it weren't for the fact she'd cared for the woman from the time she pinned cloth rectangles onto her bottom, and that their relationship had matured into friendship, Miss Jenny would have probably fired her long ago. "Really, Marylu, can't you just greet our visitor?"

Marylu snorted. The man was someone she'd never laid eyes on, to be sure, but any courtesy Jenny's admonition drummed up fled when the man lifted a booted foot and stared straight at her, a challenge in his dark eyes.

"You full of pepper, but you'll land on your backside out this door if you set that dirty boot on my clean floor."

Miss Jenny stopped at the edge of the wet floor to speak. "Can I help you?"

The customer's gaze shifted, and he lowered his booted foot to the dry spot within the front door. He lifted his hands, palms up, then shrugged. His mouth opened then closed.

When he rolled his gaze to Marylu, the realization dawned on her slow and sure. She'd heard of people being deaf and unable to talk, but the man could obviously hear.

Without prompting, he opened his mouth, eyes rounding, a manic, evil gleam sharpening his gaze and turning his eyes almost black.

Miss Jenny gasped and took a step back.

Marylu watched the man closely. "He can't talk," she said for the benefit of her employer. Still, she took a step closer to Jenny to offer the woman her protection should the man be a lunatic after all. Best safe than a name in the *Greencastle Press*'s obituaries.

The man's head bobbed in agreement to Marylu's observation. He returned to his pantomime, hands raised, fingers like talons, the dark, coarse material of his shirt giving them a detached life of their own. The pale palms wrapped around his neck.

Miss Jenny's cold hand grasped Marylu's.

"He's not crazy." Marylu hoped mightily she was on target with that statement. "Watch him close. He's telling his story."

His eyes took on something akin to terror and desperation, as the hands seemed to bend him backward. One released his neck and hovered over his open mouth, making a quick slicing gesture. An awful gagging sound emanated from him.

Miss Jenny didn't loosen her grip until the man's hands went back to his sides and he straightened, his face once again emotionless.

Marylu felt weak at what she'd witnessed. "Your tongue was cut out," she stated in a flat tone.

His nod made her stomach heave at the vileness of such a thing.

His eyes held a twinkle that sparked brighter. His gaze on her felt like hot sunshine after a cold rain.

Marylu felt warmth slide along her arms and across her chest, in a way she had never felt warmed. She broke away from those probing eyes and rubbed her stomach. Probably just indigestion from the plate of eggs she'd gobbled down that morning.

"What can we do for you?" Miss Jenny asked.

"Least you can do is offer up a name," Marylu suggested in a hard, impatient tone.

But despite the hard clip to her voice, his brown eyes never wavered from her. He raised his hands to his chest and patted. His lips moved to shape two syllables.

Marylu watched in spite of herself and caught on right away to what he was trying to express. "Chest-er. Um-hm. You must be right proud of yourself thinking up a way to tell people that one."

He sent her a melodramatic wink that nevertheless rolled a pleasing sensation through the pit of her stomach. Maybe it wasn't that cold fried egg after all.

Miss Jenny snapped her fingers. "Chester Jones! You're here to pick up the order for Mrs. Lease. She mentioned sending someone over."

Chester's grin went huge, and he nodded, showing a set of bright whites.

"Let me get that for you." Jenny did an about-face and disappeared into the storage area. Chester's attention swung back to Marylu, starting another strange roiling in her stomach. She tried to ignore the intensity of his gaze and focused, instead, on the huge chip on his right front tooth. "Miss McGreary'll get your order right off, but you don't set one foot on this here clean floor."

Chester's lips pressed together in ill-concealed mirth and he lifted his very muddy booted foot, eyes daring her.

Marylu gave him a hard frown.

He took a step forward, eyes locked on her. Then he took another. Crumbles of mud left vague outlines of his boots on the planks.

"You get!" Marylu lunged and yanked up the broom she'd used earlier. She lifted it high and swung it.

Chester put his hands up as the broom came down.

"Marylu!"

She froze, lowered the broom, and waited for her employer to chastise her further.

Chester's eyes were as wide as his smile.

"He's picking up an order for a customer," Miss Jenny reminded in the gentle tone that stirred remembrances of her mother's.

Chester bent and slapped his knee. A coarse sound issued from his throat, the unmistakable garble of laughter.

"I'm sorry, Miss Jenny," Marylu said, all the while her fingers itching to give the man another dose of the broom.

Jenny handed the package over to Chester and walked him to the door.

Mud fell off his boots in chunks now. Clutching his package

to his chest, he turned and looked beyond Miss Jenny and straight into Marylu's eyes. He winked at her and left.

When the door closed behind him, Miss Jenny turned and stared at Marylu, a strange look in her pale blue eyes.

Marylu set the broom aside. "What you thinkin' on so hard?"

"I've never seen you act that way before."

"Never had a man so ornery before."

"No, no. I mean, there's a glow about you. . . ." Miss Jenny smirked and crossed her arms. "I think I hear the popping of grease in a hot skillet."

two

Marylu rolled to her side. Sleep would not come. Maple syrup eyes and a grin full of vinegar kept invading her thoughts and making her heart beat harder. She sure liked what she'd seen of the man, but Miss Jenny's comment rubbed her wrong. Hot grease indeed!

She squeezed her eyes shut and willed her body to relax. In only a few hours she would need to be at Antrim House, a hotel across the street from Jenny's dress shop, cleaning up the rooms.

Upstairs.

Twelve steps.

Her knees ached just thinking on it.

Her right knee did better than her left, what with the injury that had happened all those years ago. Scrubbing floors always woke up the pain. Shifting positions didn't help ease the hurt neither. She decided to get herself up and start on breakfast. Miss Jenny wasn't a big eater, but the rest of the "family," as Jenny liked to call them, could put away some food. Old Cooper ate like a man condemned to death and scheduled to hang.

Marylu lumbered into the kitchen and worked some firewood into the box of the cookstove. A light shuffling made her jump and spin.

Cooper White stumped his way to the table and sat down.

"Good morning to you too, old man."

Cooper lifted drooping eyes to Marylu. "None of your lip, woman. Why don't you get some coffee going?"

"I ain't your woman."

"Could be."

Marylu crossed her arms, invigorated by the morning word

toss. "Not till I'm stiff and cold."

"I don't figure I have long to wait then—you being as cold-hearted as they come."

She flicked open the coffeepot as much to check its contents as to hide the grin erupting. Cooper was ancient. Near to fifty-five by her best guess. If she married him, she wouldn't have to wait long to be a widow. But a year over thirty didn't mean she was desperate, her only regret being she'd probably not see any beautiful black babies of her own. Sobered a bit by the sad thought, she pointed at the empty water bucket. "You scoot yourself and get some water."

Cooper got to his feet, slow as a slug in salt. He returned as she finished grinding the coffee beans and set the full bucket on a stool. "Now can I get some coffee?"

Marylu ladled some water into the coffeepot, added the grounds, and set it to heat. "You'd think you'd have learned yourself some patience by now." She used a linen to protect her hand and opened the firebox to stick in a couple more pieces of wood.

"Too old to be patient. Gotta hurry and get things done before no more time's to be had."

Marylu wiped her hands and sat down across from Cooper. "You still getting your night scares?"

He lifted tired eyes to hers. "I'll never forget that time. Thought that man was gonna shoot us dead. Then when he didn't and he told us we was going south, I wished he would have."

Marylu sat up straighter. "Seeing you all was the hardest thing. . ." The silence stretched long between them. Images of that night fifteen years ago flared to life in Marylu's head.

The wagon had rolled into Greencastle upon the Confederates' retreat from Gettysburg, full of black-skinned strangers with fear in their eyes and guards surrounding them. Marylu remembered watching Miss Jenny's mama and papa taking in the pitiful sight. She also knew, before they ever started whispering, that they were forming a plan to help the blacks, just as they, for years, had helped those who came to them in the night to escape to the North.

"You were a brave woman," Cooper interrupted her thoughts. "When that horse reared up, I thought you was done for, but you just did what it took."

"Except where those hooves snapped on my knee. Still aches."

Cooper nodded. "Reminder of what you done. Brave woman. Still are. Got more sass than most. Guess living with Miss Jenny's family made you feel that brave."

Marylu dropped her hand to the table and speared Cooper with her eyes. "Not brave. I just knew what was right. There'd been enough suffering from them Rebs looting the stores as they came through town the first time. Had all our people runnin' farther up north."

"Those of us still 'round won't ever forget what you done." Cooper's eyes took on a faraway gleam. "When you came out right under that chaplain's nose with Miss Jenny's daddy and that other man. . ." He shook his head.

She wrestled for something to distract Cooper from the subject of that night and the wagon full of slaves she'd help to free. Only God's strength had helped her then, as it helped her now. No matter how the slaves had hailed her as their hero and dubbed her "Queenie," she had only done what had to be done. The fact that she'd lost her heart in the process didn't matter none. Most had forgotten Walter. He was a moon that would never rise again, and Marylu didn't want to think on him. Didn't do any good. Just like taking the reverence to heart of those that she had helped free didn't leave her quite comfortable.

Cooper slapped his leg. "I told the whole story to Chester, and he just smiled and nodded like he does—"

Marylu's back snapped erect. "Chester?"

Cooper chuckled. "That's right. The mute. He wanted to meet you real bad. Said he'd heard the story even way down in South Carolina about a black woman freeing her own."

She ignored that and focused on his apparent familiarity with the black man. "Mute he might be, but he can hear just fine."

"Heard he stomped on your floor and got your temper to flarin' pretty hot." He slapped his leg. "Wished I'd seen that. Not often a man gets one over on you." Cooper loosed a chuckle. "He was right impressed with you and the story of you saving all of us, Queenie."

Marylu frowned. "Don't call me that. I was as scared as you all were that night." She cast an eye toward the coffeepot and used it as an excuse to move from the table.

"And what about them years you worked in the railroad?"

"Miss Jenny's papa did that. Was my job to keep Miss Jenny safe."

"That's not the way Miss Jenny tells it."

"She wasn't even eight when we started. You taking her word over mine?" Marylu poured coffee into two tin cups and set one in front of Cooper. "Don't you have a garden to tend or something?"

Cooper eyed the window and the peek of sunlight lightening the sky more with each passing minute. "Guess so. Good time to work when the heat's not so much."

As the older man sipped on his coffee, Marylu realized her only way to learn more about Chester was to pry it out of Cooper. The trick was to do it without his knowing she wanted to know. "How'd you find out that Chester muddied my floor?"

Cooper's smile showed few signs of teeth. "Told me. Not so much with words as with his hands and face. He's something else."

"Where'd he come from?"

The older man scratched his scantily bearded face. "Jumped him a boxcar and road in. Got himself some kin hereabouts."

"Kin? Up here? What'd he go down south for then?"

Cooper cocked a brow at her. "Why you so interested?"

Marylu puffed up. "Ain't interested a speck. Can't a body

make some conversation? He's new in town. Don't that stir the curiosity of most?"

Cooper slapped his leg and spit a laugh.

She snapped a hard look at him, which made him laugh all the harder. "Ain't you got a garden to hoe?"

Cooper got himself vertical in a painful unfolding that took a full minute to happen. He'd been worked hard in the fields all those years before escaping north. It made him seem older than he really was. But he didn't complain. His eyes took on a gleam as he looped a finger through his coffee mug. "I'll let Chester know you're wanting to know about him."

"You best not, Cooper White."

The sound of his laughter dimmed only when the door shut behind him.

❧

Chester Jones shook the water from his head and buried his face in the towel. The water felt good to his skin. It was a welcome contrast to the warm pond water in the South where he used to do all his bathing under the mammoth branches of an ancient oak, streaming with moss.

He eyed himself in the mirror of the washstand. No matter how much he dabbed his face with water, he'd never be able to wash away the redness brimming his eyes. He shivered as the sounds of his dream twisted and taunted his mind. A familiar dream that by turns kept him awake or shattered a sound sleep.

Lord, help me. Cleanse me of these scares. Clean me up.

Clean like the days before he'd left home seeking a life apart from his mama and siblings. No use sticking around when they had all those mouths to feed. He'd made himself believe that was his only reason for leaving. Truth had come with maturity and suffering. Reality being he'd left because he was nine parts rebellious and one part wanting to scratch the itch to travel.

He'd been a fool to leave the only security he'd known all his life, all the promise that his yesterdays and his youth had held. Staying north would have saved him the stripes on his back and the long hours in the fields, but he hadn't listened to his mama. Hadn't allowed himself to soften at her crestfallen expression when he'd announced his decision to leave home. In his head, he could still see the hurt in her eyes. The fear. All for him. If he had expected tears at his announcement, he should have known better, for his mama was too strong a woman to spill salt all over the place, no matter the depth of the heartache.

I failed her, too, didn't I?

He filled his lungs and released the breath in a long, measured exhale. Was no use talking to God. No use talking at all anymore. But he'd come to this state to see his mama and sister, the only kin he knew of, the rest scattered by his father's sudden death. His family's noble sacrifice for the North that his father loved, fought, and died for as part of the 54th Massachusetts Volunteer Regiment.

He died a braver man than me.

Chester straightened and tried to shake off the gloom that permeated his mind. He had to put the past behind him and figure out a better way to get people to understand him. Some understood him better than others. Like the fine woman he'd seen in the dress shop. Surely she had sass aplenty. He'd heard many stories of how she'd set free a wagon full of slaves captured in Gettysburg. Even on the run he'd heard the stories. Among blacks, stories of heroism were transferred from one wagging tongue to another, faster than any mail service.

He had delayed heading west to Mercersburg, where his mama and sister lived, in order to meet Marylu Biloxi. Chance had brought him face-to-face with Cooper the day he'd gotten off the train. It had taken Chester a week to discover that the man knew Marylu. He even lived in a little house out back of the one Marylu lived in with her friend and employer, Jenny McGreary. As soon as Cooper discovered his passion for building furniture and such, the old man had taken him straight to the owner of Antrim House and got him a job. Mr. Shillito's recent purchase of the hotel, and his plans to renovate, meant job security.

Chester shifted his weight and squinted out the window of his little room on the first floor of Antrim House. He reviewed his meeting with Marylu. He had been surprised at her beauty. High cheekbones. Moonlit-night skin that set off the glow in her eyes, the color of a golden pancake. But her sass had brought his smile out of hiding, and once he felt the grin on his lips, it seemed he couldn't stop smiling. His spirits had lifted and soared. A feeling he'd not felt for a long time.

He blinked and reached for his worn shirt, buttoning it on as he crossed the room. He needed to get started on the tables and chairs Mr. Shillito had requested. He finished the last buttonhole and swung the door wide.

A woman stood in the hallway, her back to him, but Chester's heart slammed against his chest as Marylu Biloxi threw a questioning glance over her shoulder. When their eyes met, she turned and put a hand to her chest. "What you doing here?"

three

Marylu dropped her hand. "You 'bout made my heart stop."

Chester took note of her bright blue dress and crisp white apron, not to mention the curves filling out the clothing in all the right places. He wondered if her statement meant his presence stirred something in her or if he'd spooked her. He donned an imaginary hat and gave her a deep bow.

"Mr. Shillito didn't tell me you were the one he'd hired."

Chester pressed his lips together and let the sparkle shine in his eyes, then punctuated the moment with a quick shrug.

"You best be knowing how to work real hard."

His mind drifted to the many scars across his back, not that he'd been afraid of work or ever caught shirking the rows in the fields down south. No, the lashes had been a matter of pleasing a very unpleasable master. He must have let the melancholy slip into his expression, because Marylu's eyes grew softer.

"I'm right sure you know all there is to know about hard work."

To this he bobbed his head. He knew about running, too. Running hard and long and trying to outpace howling dogs on four legs. He knew the racing heart and the prickle of cold sweat and the twist of dread that clinched the gut tighter as each howl got closer and the voices of his pursuers louder.

She put a hand on his arm, and he gave himself a mental shake.

"Make a list of what you need to make room five right again. Drunk man smashed it up pretty bad, and Mr. Shillito wants it put right."

Chester stood straight as a stick, stuck out his chest, and saluted.

She frowned and mocked anger. "Don't you be forgettin' it either, or I'll have your hide."

He watched her go, aware of her in a way that was sure to bring him trouble. How could he think for a minute to pin his hopes of settling down on a woman whose soul showed more bravery and courage than he could ever hope to muster?

The man was haunted, to be sure. Marylu knew the interpretation of the expression on Chester's face. She'd seen it a thousand times as she'd helped Miss Jenny's father feed the slaves that came to them on those dark nights, long ago. Pain and suffering. Fear so deep it cut her to witness it.

Something else tweaked at her mind. The sight of the faint red around his eyes. She knew what that meant, too. Had seen it too many times in Cooper after he'd spent a long, sleepless night, rocked by his nightmares of the days he'd spent down south.

She pushed the broom she held into the corners of room three and chased a spider away in the process. After Marylu finished cleaning the first four rooms and entered room five, she was amazed to find most of the repairs already taken care of.

Chester hunched over a broken chair, his thick fingers assessing the smoothness of the new chair leg he was sanding. He placed the chair on the floor and braced his hands on corners diagonal from each other and rocked the piece to see if it wobbled. Marylu grinned when she saw that it remained stable and level. Face lit with satisfaction, Chester got to his feet and smoothed down his spiking hair.

"You need a shearing," she observed.

His eyes glowed, and he ran a hand over his hair and stirred it into a wild fan around his head.

Marylu shook her head at his antics, reached out, and pressed it back down. The springy feel of his hair startled her somehow and stirred her to a heightened awareness of the intimacy of the gesture. She snatched her hand away and swallowed over the sudden ache in her throat. "You get on over to the McGrearys' tonight, and I'll sharpen my shears and fix you up."

His eyes rounded, and took on the look of an excited puppy. He rubbed a hand over his midsection.

"I'm guessing I can find something to feed you as well." With all his hand-waving, even if born of necessity, he must work up an appetite. But how did he eat without a tongue? She wondered, too, if he got tired of trying to communicate everything with his hands and gestures. To have to be quick to act out everything he wanted to say, not to mention patient enough to wait for the person he talked with to interpret what he meant. It must make him feel very isolated. "Cooper says he knows you, that you got kin 'round here."

His nod came slow, and the sadness returned to pull his face into a frown.

She wondered why he hadn't moved on to see his family already. "You not here to raise trouble, are you?"

He shook his head.

"See that you don't. We don't like rabble-rousers. We got ourselves a church. You do church, don't you?"

His eyes went round and dull for a fleeting minute but lightened into a gentle glow, accompanied by an enthusiastic nod. He spread his arms wide as if to take in the whole room then pointed to the chair he had been working on. His puppy eyes locked on hers, and he raised his brows.

"You did a fine job, Chester." She folded her arms and grunted. "But if you ever dare to walk across any floor of mine with your muddy boots again, I'll pluck you bald one hair at a time."

Chester gave a look of mock horror and covered his head with his hands.

Marylu bit down hard, but a single laugh squeezed through. Chester's laughter joined hers, until both of them were gasping for breath.

That bit of merrymaking sustained Marylu through the long morning. Chester, too, seemed lighter of spirit when she left to go to McGreary's Dress Shop in the afternoon. Announcing herself as she opened the back door of Miss Jenny's shop, Marylu hadn't moved three full paces through the back door when Miss Jenny stuck her head out of the nearby storage area.

Jenny's huge grin mirrored the look she had given Marylu the previous day when making her hot grease comment. "I don't guess I have to ask what has you so cheery looking. I heard Levitt Burns's wife whispering something about the 'mute,' as she called him."

"That's full nonsense."

"The 'mute' part or that Mrs. Burns was whispering?"

Marylu sent her a look.

Her friend's smile spread from ear to ear. "Mrs. Burns will be in later today to drop off some mending and order some new dresses. I'll let her know you said she was full of nonsense."

"Wouldn't do you good to open your mouth at all. She wouldn't let you drop one word before she trampled you 'neath a mouthful of her own."

Miss Jenny juggled two bolts of cloth. "So you didn't see him?"

"I saw him."

"It's good to see you so happy."

"Ain't no happier than usual."

Miss Jenny giggled in response, clearly unconvinced, and passed the bolts of cloth to Marylu. "These need to go out on the table, and then the hem needs to be put in Miss Rosaleigh's wedding dress."

Glad for a change in topic, Marylu plucked the bolts from her employer's arms. "You finished her bonnet?"

"It came together nicely this morning. Good thing, too, because I've got to start on Mrs. Carl's order."

"You're working awful hard."

Jenny paused in pinning a pattern to smooth blue cotton.

"It helps fill the hours. If not for you and Cooper, I don't know what I'd do for company." She smoothed the wrinkles in the paper and continued pinning.

"You could give Aaron a chance. That Sally is a little too flighty for him. Pay him some attention, and he'll be sure to notice."

Scissors appeared in Miss Jenny's hand. She gave a practice *snip-snip* then set to work cutting around the edges of the pattern. Marylu waited for a response, surprised when none came, not even a blatant denial of the suggestion.

They worked at their respective tasks for more than an hour, interrupted when Mrs. Burns entered the store, cheeks flushed and hair slipping down from the combs, forming ringlets around her face.

"Good afternoon, Mrs. Burns." Marylu watched Miss Jenny welcome the woman. They conferred on materials for a good ten minutes before Jenny faced her. "Could you lay out some patterns for Mrs. Burns, Marylu? I've got to get this dress basted."

Marylu did as instructed, laying out the patterns on the long display case, as Mrs. Burns expressed interest.

"It's good to see you so well, Marylu," Mrs. Burns commented.

"Thank ya, ma'am."

The woman drew in a great breath, and Marylu braced herself for the verbal flood headed her way, wishing she was Moses and could part the waters before the flood drowned her.

"I was just telling Jenny the other day how lucky she was to have such a faithful and devoted servant in you. I know how much comfort you and Cooper bring to her. It's a shame she can't find a suitable companion. Of course, I did hear that Aaron down at the mill was looking her way, until Sally Worth wore that azure dress last Sunday and sashayed around him until he finally asked her to the church picnic. Though I'm sure you wouldn't have known about that since you have your own church. You should be having a new member, too. Mr. Shillito hired that mute man who came into town. You seen him?"

Marylu didn't even bother molding her tongue around a reply.

"I'm sure you did," Mrs. Burns answered her own question. "He's a quiet one to be sure, but I guess that's because of his tongue being cut. Not all of it from what I hear, but enough to make it impossible for him to form most letters. A shame, I'm sure, but right punishment for a murderer, don't you think?"

four

"It can't be true." Miss Jenny's mouth pursed. She gave the scissors a snip into the air to punctuate the statement. "He doesn't look the type."

"Since when are you one to judge on looks?" Marylu unfolded the large section of material her employer was set to begin cutting.

"Oh, I don't. He just seems so"—she bent over the table, her brows creased—"gentle."

Marylu didn't answer. Couldn't answer, truth be told, because it was the exact word she would have used to describe Chester Jones's appearance. Sure, he got sassy with her, but his eyes held a quietness that seemed to show an inner strength. Her skin tightened, and gooseflesh rose along her arms. But that description could fit a lot of men. And she had been wrong before. Maybe Chester wasn't gentle. Those red-rimmed eyes might hide a deeper problem, and she herself had felt he looked tormented at least once during their morning exchange.

She sighed. No use fussin' around with thoughts of him anyhow. What with Miss Jenny pinning on the pattern, there was work to be done. Marylu smoothed her hand over the fabric, and she recalled the impulsive touch of her hand upon his hair earlier.

"You're blushing, Marylu." Jenny's eyes sparkled with pure mischief.

Miffed at having been caught woolgathering about the man, again, she opened her mouth then closed it with a snap.

"You look like a fish!" Jenny's laughter tinkled across the table that separated them.

Heat rose up Marylu's neck and fanned into her cheeks. She pressed her hands to the warmth and averted her face.

Jenny's mirth stuttered to a stop. "I'm sorry. It's just that I don't ever get to see you so flustered, and I, well, I couldn't resist."

Marylu felt her friend's light touch on her shoulder and raised her head.

"There's something about him, isn't there?" Her friend's eyes were serious now.

Marylu didn't respond. Didn't want to. Days ago she would have called herself or anyone else four kinds of fool for thinking there would ever be another man to pique her interest. Now she wasn't so sure.

But Chester, a murderer? If nothing else, she wanted to know his story. Mrs. Burns's wagging tongue did little to convince her that Chester was indeed guilty of taking someone else's life. Besides, she had long ago learned it best not to believe something until she heard it straight from the source.

Jenny picked up the edge of the material and poised to make the first cut. "You know that Mrs. Burns sometimes gets things wrong."

It was as if Jenny had read her mind. Though her friend's words were a much kinder explanation of Mrs. Burns's motive than she would have offered up. "I'll be making sure of the story. You can count on it."

&

Cooper opened his big trap as soon as Marylu stepped through the door and into the kitchen.

"Heard you've got yourself some butchering to do tonight."

She raised a brow and spun a circle at her ear with an index finger. "You finally gone plumb crazy. What butchering?"

Cooper ran a hand over his close-cropped, more-scalp-than-anything hair. "Hair butchering. Chester was wide-eyed over the idea of coming here this evening. If that boy could talk proper, he'd have been spilling words all afternoon."

She paused to absorb this, secretly pleased but not for a moment going to let it show. She moved aside as Miss Jenny rustled through the door behind her.

Cooper creaked himself vertical and reached out to take Miss Jenny's packages.

"Why thank you, Cooper."

"Why sure. Can't let a pretty gal like yourself tote around heavy things."

Marylu snorted. "You let me do it often enough."

Cooper slapped the package down onto the table. "I said 'pretty gal.' You needin' your hearing checked?"

It only took her a second to yank up the heavy iron skillet and wave it threateningly.

Jenny stepped between them.

"Don't you get in the way, Miss Jenny. I'm going to give him what he has coming."

"Marylu, really. A fine example of Christianity you are."

"I am. The good Lord expects us to fight the devil. Now let me at him."

Cooper doubled up and slapped a hand to his thigh.

Jenny shook her head, but the smile broke through. "What would I do without you two to keep me on my toes?"

Marylu lowered the skillet. "I can think of a few things I could do without him around."

Cooper folded himself onto the bench and started up coughing.

Jenny sat beside him, a hand on his shoulder. "You need me to call the doctor?"

"I've got some good strong medicine for him," Marylu inserted. "Cure him of every bit of meanness ailing him. 'Course, it would cure him stiff and cold."

"How can you be so mean to me?" Cooper raised his watery eyes to meet hers.

Marylu huffed, admitted that he didn't look too good, and then relented. "I'll get you some tea."

He coughed real hard. "Lots of honey."

"I've made you hundreds of cups of tea in your life, and you're going to sit there and act like I don't know how you like it?" Marylu suspected Miss Jenny would coo over him a bit longer. She had a soft spot for the old man. Marylu set about cutting up roast and chopping vegetables for a stew. When the water for the tea came to a boil, Marylu got down the honey and began fixing three cups.

For all the drama Cooper could drum up, their little ritual of taking tea, and reading the Bible at the end of the work-day, never failed to bring its own brand of comfort. They were a mismatched family, to be sure, but they loved each other.

She loved Cooper even more when he was quiet, though she had to admit that cough had her worried. The sound seemed raw, and she pondered the idea of putting some crushed garlic into his tea to ward off any further sickness.

When she set the teacups out, a thick silence settled around the room, disturbed only by the vague crackling of the wood fire fueling the stove. Cooper seemed content to warm his hands around the hot cup, his gaze distant. Jenny stirred her tea absently, as if Marylu hadn't quite worked the sugar into the amber liquid, but she guessed the woman had her mind on business, or a dress or bonnet.

Marylu slipped down on the bench, not realizing until she got still how much her body needed the rest. Muscles seemed to unbunch, and her knee protested being bent after so many hours. She inhaled the steam and wished she'd put a pinch of cinnamon into her cup, but the prospect of rising didn't appeal in the least, so she contented herself with sipping the tea plain.

"Guess we'd best be reading before the night gets away from us." Marylu grunted and reached toward the Bible sitting in its usual place at the end of the table. No dust collecting on this Bible. Not with Cooper to keep in line, a task made all the lighter since he almost always deferred to her and Miss Jenny to do the reading.

The leather cover of the Bible had begun to crack from the years of wear. Marylu ran a finger down the fracture and wondered if the local bookbinder could do something to mend the tear. The Bible had been a gift to them from Jenny's mama and daddy, and she sure and certain wanted to keep it in good repair.

"You gonna read or start to bawling?" Cooper frowned, though his eyes held a mischievous gleam. A cough choked him up, followed by another.

"You just worry about sucking down that tea. You hear?"

Miss Jenny put a hand to Cooper's shoulder. "I really think I should fetch the doctor."

"I'm an old man," he barked, the words punctuated with another cough. "If I gotta go, no doctor's gonna prevent it."

Marylu flipped the pages to Samuel. "And we're surely not going to stand in the way, either."

"Honestly!" Jenny sent Marylu a stern look. "The two of you are just terrible."

Cooper balled a fist and pressed it to his lips as if to stifle another cough. Marylu saw the gesture for what it was worth, a ploy to cover his amusement. The man's dark, watery eyes met hers long enough to deliver a wink, before another cough yanked at his chest.

Jenny didn't notice the exchange, unconsciously patting the man on the back as the coughing fit continued.

Such a straying of attention made Marylu hold her finger underneath the verse she'd been about to read and frown. Miss Jenny's stare wasn't directed at the cookstove in an I-need-to-get-a-new-one kind of way. No, her eyes were focused on something Marylu couldn't see, and she had a feeling she knew what had her employer and friend so distracted. What *man* had her so distracted, to be exact.

Marylu ran her finger down the Bible passage they were to read that evening and wondered how best to approach the subject of Aaron Walck. The man had captured Miss Jenny's fancy soon after the death of his wife, and it seemed, to Marylu's mind, that Jenny's interest hadn't waned a bit.

"Are you going to begin, Marylu?" Miss Jenny asked.

"Got it right here. First Samuel 18." As she read out loud,

the verses became mere words, so caught up was she in trying to make sense of Miss Jenny's preoccupation.

"This is such a sad story. Saul started out with such promise and slid away into such bitterness," Jenny murmured.

Marylu gave an absent nod. "Spirit gets hold of a person and don't let go."

"He made bad choices," Jenny added.

"Reminds me of that young Zedikiah. He best be getting some sense in that head of his before his brains shrink up." Marylu opened her mouth to add something more to the statement but closed it.

Miss Jenny's gaze had sought out Cooper's and something passed between them. Cooper wasted no time in starting up a coughing fit, but Marylu knew she'd missed some silent message. A message that looked much like a gentle rebuke.

five

For the next hour they ate and talked about Saul. Miss Jenny seemed inclined to have her say about the man's change of heart and his ability to sire a young man like Jonathan, who had a soft heart despite his father. And all the while, Marylu listened to Miss Jenny's soliloquy with rising suspicion.

Cooper seemed bent on studying the ingredients of the stew and the rim of his bowl. She wanted to stop her friend and ask what was going on but thought it best to hold her tongue.

It wasn't long after Cooper had shuffled his empty bowl to the counter that Miss Jenny seemed satisfied and closed the subject.

When Jenny left to work on some mending for Cooper, Marylu whirled on him. "What was that all about? I saw her giving you messages with her eyes."

"To know me is to love me."

"That's not the kind of eyeballing she was giving you, and you know it."

Cooper's shoulders slumped, and a sigh further deflated his frame. "It's an old problem."

"I'm listening."

The old man didn't raise his face or even twitch. Marylu's stomach twisted. She could remember only a handful of times ever seeing Cooper cry, and they were always like this. He'd get real quiet and still and then haul the handkerchief from his back pocket and take a swipe at his eyes and snort into the cloth. All the signs tears were there.

He crammed the kerchief back into his pocket and finally raised his face to her. "You think you know all 'bout me, but you don't. Sometimes a body's done too many wrongs and

32

ain't nothing no one can do to help."

Whatever it was, it had to be bad. She twisted it over in her head how it was that Jenny knew something about old Cooper she didn't. The revelation seemed a recent one, making it all the more mysterious. Cooper hardly ever went anywhere or did anything out of his routine.

She turned her back on the man and set to work on the dishes. A light knock on the door broke the rhythm of swishing her rag around the plate. She glanced over her shoulder to make sure Cooper would break from his doldrums to open the door.

"Good to have some man-company for a change," she heard Cooper greet their visitor.

Marylu set aside the clean dish. "I'll get my shears out in a minute. Let me finish up these dishes. You had yourself some supper, Chester?"

Not only did she not expect an answer, she didn't wait for one. Plucking a bowl from the open cabinet, she ladled stew into it. No bachelor she knew would cook for himself unless held at gunpoint.

When she turned, bowl in hand, she met Chester's gaze. He stood at the closed door as if afraid to enter the room, or unsure of himself, though his eyes held the light of a man full of sass.

Marylu's hair prickled along her scalp. She slid the bowl down the table, careful not to spill any, and motioned Chester to take his seat. "Got more where that came from if you've a mind for it."

Chester took a hesitant step toward the bench, then stopped and lifted an eyebrow first to Cooper then to her.

"We already ate." She pointed at the open Bible. "We were spending some time in the Word. You be sure not to splash on the pages."

She didn't stay to watch him eat, afraid the sight might be more than she could handle. Mrs. Burns's words came back to her. Yet Chester's soft eyes that held such fascination for her seemed incapable of hatred. She might as well just admit that he had a way about him that she found appealing.

Marylu stretched upward and retrieved the scissors she used to cut cloth and snip hair off Cooper when she couldn't stand looking at the bush on his head a minute longer. Though hair on that man's head hadn't been a problem for the last ten years or so. It fell out faster than it grew.

When she returned to the table, Cooper sat chatting in a low voice to Chester, telling him of life in the area since the great battle at Gettysburg. Chester listened with interest, his bowl not nearly as empty as she expected. She forced herself to watch him spoon some into his mouth. Nothing drooled out the sides. He seemed to take a bit longer to chew and work things around, but other than that, nothing out of the ordinary. She almost sighed her relief then wondered why it mattered so much.

She worked the scissors in her right hand, the sharp snap gaining the attention of both men. Smile lines appeared beside Chester's eyes as he chewed.

"You sharpen these like I asked you?" She directed the question at Cooper.

"Sure did. Sharpened them real good."

She nodded, and with nothing left to do but wait, she sat herself down across from the two men and pulled the Bible close to read more about Saul. And to give herself some time to gather her wits before putting her fingers in the hair of the man who had captured her interest so easily.

๛

Chester did his best to keep his eyes on his stew or on Cooper's face, but every time Marylu moved from one place to another, he knew he must be giving himself away. Cooper didn't seem inclined to tease him none, but Chester didn't want to let down his guard.

She captivated him. He imagined he could see the nobility of her character in the fine shape of her nose and the squareness of her jaw. Tendrils of hair popped out from beneath the kerchief she wore on her head and got him to wondering what it would be like to see her without the covering. Was her hair tinged with gray? Would it be curly and short or longer and pulled back?

He didn't miss the fine stitching of the dress she wore or the little details that spoke of a woman good with a needle and with access to fine materials. At least finer than most of the women he knew.

He dipped his spoon and stirred the savory stew, inhaling deeply of the rich scent of beef and potatoes. The woman could cook, though he'd never doubted it for a minute with all the stories of her he'd heard.

When she snipped the scissors and questioned Cooper, he allowed himself the opportunity to savor every bit of her appearance without the worry of Cooper seeing his admiration. He swallowed the bite of potato he'd been working on and wondered what she thought of him. Did she see a strong man or a coward?

He fastened his attention on spooning up another morsel of stew. It didn't matter what she saw. He knew the truth. A woman like Marylu could never admire a man like him, and probably the rumors of his past had reached her by now, swollen with speculation and rife with inconsistencies, but the basic truth was there.

The very thought clenched his stomach, and he knew the tremors would prevent him from taking another bite. He fisted his hands and dug them into his lap, willing the trembling to stop before it started.

He stabbed a quick glance across the table at Marylu, relieved to see her attention on the Bible in front of her. But Cooper noticed, the old eyes probing deeply into his. They sat, gazes clenched, for minutes before Cooper moved his head in a slow nod. Chester didn't know what the gesture meant, but the old man braced his hand and rose slowly from the table.

"I think Chester's ready for those scissors."

Marylu's head snapped up. "You stay put, and I'll work you over, too."

Cooper shook his head. "Not me. I've got myself a project to work on." He ran a hand over his grizzled hair and favored Chester with a smile that looked more like a grimace. "Don't let her get too much of your scalp."

"You get out of here," Marylu spat. "I've shorn more old goats like you than sheep. Chester at least won't give me any lip."

Cooper's dry chuckle was punctuated by a stale cough as he opened the door.

"You shouldn't be out in that night air with that cough."

Cooper didn't reply. The door shut, leaving only a cold draft of air to wash over Chester.

Marylu shivered. "Don't know why that man can't listen to me for once." She stood in profile to him, lost in thought, gaze on the door that Cooper had disappeared through, unconsciously opening and closing the scissors she held.

Chester rubbed at his chin. Honestly, he couldn't imagine it either. For a moment he lost himself in what it would feel like to be looked after by a woman. Any woman. But especially Marylu.

Another snap of the scissors and she startled from her reverie and turned toward him. "You sit still now and I'll get to work. No use me worrying over that man. He sure doesn't worry himself over his body's needs."

Chester nodded and figured it better to agree. At least while she held a pair of scissors.

six

Cooper's doings shrank away as Marylu set about snipping at Chester's head. She brushed his hair back with her fingers to gauge the evenness of her cuts then trimmed some more. The mostly black hair fell at her feet, looking like miniature balls of coarse yarn.

He sensed the way he needed to turn his head to accommodate her cutting, which pleased Marylu. When she ran her fingers through the ever-shortening mop, she became more aware of the intimacy of the gesture and all she had missed being unmarried. She swallowed hard over the swell of grief.

If things had worked out all those years ago, she might very well be cutting the hair of her own man instead of every stray Cooper brought in. Rather than allow that line of thinking to distract her, she grasped for some subject to chat about, but the notion shattered when the question burned through her mind, *So, did you really kill someone?* If he said yes, she just might go down on her knees and take to crying. And her knees hurt too much already for that to happen. If only there was some way to communicate with him.

She froze mid-snip. Her gaze fell on the cupboard above the bucket of water. If Chester wondered why the steady snipping motion stopped, he didn't react.

Marylu slipped the scissors into her pocket and crossed the room. Yanking open the cupboard door, she lifted onto her toes and slid her hand along the rough wood of the top shelf. Her fingertips grazed a cool, smooth surface, and she withdrew the object and faced Chester, holding the board up for him to see.

His head tilted at her, brow lowered in concentration. It was a reaction she hadn't expected.

37

She stroked the smooth surface of the slate and guessed the answer to her next question, but asked it anyhow. "Do you know how to write?"

Chester lowered his gaze to his hands, as if the answer lay somewhere within the rough cuticles and broken nails. It was a reaction she had seen often in the generation that had sampled the poison of slavery.

"Then I'll teach you."

His head popped up.

Marylu witnessed the doubt that shifted into a glimmer of hope. She nodded. "I've done it before. Many times in fact. Miss Jenny made sure my family could read and cipher. I pass that on when and where I can."

ↆ

Chester felt a gentle hand squeeze his heart. Conviction shone from Marylu's eyes, turning them soft and gentle. He basked in what he saw reflected there, a surge of gratefulness carrying with it a flow of peace that washed over his heart and through his mind.

She brought the slate with her and passed it across to him. "You take that and use this to write with." She skirted the table and bent down, her face inches from his, though her full attention was on the slate.

His heart raced as her profile was silhouetted against the lantern farther down the table. He could see the texture of her skin, smooth and soft. Warmth emanated from her, enveloping him and lighting his imagination with what it would be like to hold her close.

"What you need to do first," her voice flowed over him, "is you need to learn how to hold this here pencil." She stroked her hand over the length of his and flattened it against the table, not for a moment realizing the affect her touch had on his senses. She cupped her hand around the pencil and showed him how the tool was moved by the fingers. "It's very simple, but I don't care how you hold it as long as you can make the letters right." She pulled his hand off the table and pressed the pencil into his palm. "Now it's your turn."

He mimicked what he'd seen her do. Her praise boosted his desire to try harder. When she showed him the motions of a letter she called A, he watched closely and repeated her bold strokes. She beamed a smile down on him that reminded him of sun-warmed Spanish moss twisting in a breeze.

She rained down a steady stream of praise as they progressed through the alphabet. Marylu sang the entire stream of letters he had just practiced writing. She pronounced each one, over and over, as she finished trimming his hair, and he worked the pencil on the slate to form the last of the vowels.

"Sharp as one of Miss Jenny's straight pins. You'll be writing books before too long."

She brushed off his shoulder, then moved across the room and replaced the shears in the cabinet. She untied her long apron and draped it across the bench seat before taking her place beside it.

Clearly, they were done. He had no more reason to stay, and it was late. He could feel the exhaustion in his bones, but his mind, too, felt the weight of all that he had accomplished.

"You take that on home with you and practice in whatever spare time you can find."

Her gaze met his. Before he could talk himself out of the gesture, he reached to cover her hand that she had rested on the table. The contact buzzed pulses of pleasure along his nerves.

She seemed startled. Eyes wide. She stared down at his hand, back at him, then jolted to her feet so fast the bench fell backward.

An immediate lump formed in his throat and swelled. He had panicked her. Her smile now became one plastered by politeness as she hovered near the door.

Chester didn't understand her reaction but knew it best to leave. He nodded his appreciation while pointing to his shortened hair and hurried out into the night, the prospect of returning to his small room leaving him hollow.

seven

It had been the first time a man had touched Marylu with tenderness since Walter's lips had pressed a kiss against her hand. In her mind she could still see Walter's dark head bent over her fingers. Feel the softness of his lips. But scratching out those tender moments was the moment he had taken a step backward and disappeared into the moonless night. Never to return.

Chester's hand, his touch, had startled her, sure, but her own reaction, that rush of exhilaration, left her afraid. She could have discounted the gesture as one of gratefulness for what they'd accomplished, for he'd been obviously enthusiastic about his progress, but it had been the dark softness in his gaze that told the truth. And she'd felt that same warmth from him the first day in the shop when he'd dared to defy her clean floors with his muddy feet.

She pulled the lantern closer and raised the glass to blow out the flame, when the door opened and Cooper slipped into the circle of lamplight.

He seemed startled by her presence.

"Just like you to sneak in like an errant schoolboy."

Cooper shrugged and melted onto the seat as if every last ounce of strength went from him in that second.

Marylu's expert ears picked up on his labored breathing. "Should be in bed, snugged up warm, not traipsing around in the cool night air with a cough like you've got. I told you that."

No response.

She moved around the table and felt his forehead. He was burning up with fever. She wished for Chester's presence and strength now to help lift the old man to bed. "Up with you.

I'll raise up Miss Jenny and send her to fetch the doctor."

"No need," his voice, thick with sickness, scared her more than anything. "I'll be fine come morning." He coughed.

"You won't be fine, because if that fever don't kill you, I might be tempted."

She put a hand on Cooper's arm and lifted, signaling he should raise himself.

He struggled to his feet and shuffled toward the back door.

"Now you get over to your little room quick-like and snuggle up in that bed. I'll bring you something hot and have Miss Jenny get the doctor."

"Doctor Kermit, not that other doctor. Old Kermit don't mind looking after us darkies so much." Cooper closed the door behind him.

She left to heat water and rustle around for some honey and the cinnamon she hoarded for special bakings and sickness. As she set about preparing the herbal tea, her mind turned again to Chester's touch then to Walter. Tears burned, but she widened her eyes and refused to release them. She lifted the cup and inhaled the cinnamon sweetness. The clutch of a memory, long buried, grabbed at her mind. Walter's fever. The way she had nursed him back to full health.

A rustling startled her, and she half-turned.

Miss Jenny stood in the doorway to the kitchen, worry etched in the lines beside her eyes. "I heard you down here mumbling to someone. Cooper?"

Marylu faced her friend, the cup in her hands.

Jenny's eyes dipped to the mug of tea she held. "He's worse?"

"Best fetch Doc Kermit. Or you can stay with him and I will. I told him to get himself to bed."

"I'll go. Bring some water to boil and make a tent. I'll leave immediately." Miss Jenny spun on her heel, but she held out a hand to stop her momentum. "He just got back?"

"Not ten minutes ago. Came in looking like a beat puppy."

"Was he alone?"

The question rattled around in Marylu's head and raised a

whole new set of questions. "He courting someone?"

"No. No, not at all. I just. . .wondered."

❧

Chester couldn't help but grin at his progress. Despite Marylu's withdrawal from him at the end of the evening, he had felt her pride in his accomplishments. He had worked over the alphabet on his slate most of the night, the slate pencil screeching with every carefully formed line and curve, until his eyes became heavy.

Indirect moonlight lit his room, and he pushed himself down deep under the covers. He wondered if Marylu lay sound asleep, or if late nights were spent in some sort of needlework, or maybe she read more from her Bible. After the long days she worked, sleep would come easy for her, he was sure. Nothing to haunt her nights, being raised up in a family that cared about the people under their roof.

He squeezed his eyes tighter and shifted position, willing away the thoughts that always invaded his mind when he lay down to sleep. An endless litany of harrowing moments spent on the run. Fearing capture. Of the cold nights and the pain of an empty belly.

Stop it!

A light scratch brought him alert. He lay still and tense. He hated mice and dreaded not only the thought of the little critters but also the bigger threat of their cousins. He tried to console himself that he'd not seen any of the furry vermin during the day.

Another scratch, followed by a muffled curse.

His mind flew. His small room was closest to the back door of Mr. Shillito's hotel. He drove back the covers and made short work of pulling his trousers on and snapping suspenders into place over his nightshirt. He opened the door of his room and peeked through the crack. He didn't need to see anyone to know the back door of the hotel gaped. A cold draft of air shot through the hallway and blew around his bare ankles.

A dark shadow leaned against the wall. Weak light indicated the outline of a slender man.

Chester caught the scent of alcohol. He moved slowly, unsure if the man posed a threat or simply couldn't function as a result of his inebriation. He would need to get the man to his room. At least this drunk was too soused to tear up things.

Chester took two steps in the man's direction before the shadow sunk down the wall and landed in a heap. Snuffles indicated the first stirrings of slumber that would, Chester had no doubt, lead to an all-out snore session. He poked the heap with his bare foot. Nothing. He reached down and grabbed the man's arm, startled to realize the form was that of a black boy. His mind flew over the possibilities. He stooped to wedge his shoulder beneath the boy's armpit and guide him to his feet.

The stranger must have woken long enough to understand what was being asked of him, as his movements became independent. Chester limped with the semiconscious man to his door, shoved it open with his toe, and barely got the boy through it before he lost his grip. He tried to catch his breath and hoped all the while that the noise he'd made didn't waken the only patron present on that floor this evening. Thank goodness they were in the room at the end of the hallway.

Chester took the time to light the two candles at either end of his room. He pulled the candleholder closer to the boy's face. He couldn't have been more than sixteen. Chester knelt beside the young man and slapped him lightly on the cheeks. He didn't get a response and really hadn't expected one. He rose and grabbed his shirt, balling it up to make a pillow for his visitor's head. Sleep would be the best thing for now.

Chester sat on the edge of his bed and stared at the too-thin form and the pants frayed around the hem. He blew out the candles, more bothered than he wanted to be by the still form of a drunken youth whose weakness for drink had him wandering around alone.

eight

"You're looking tired." Marylu swept Chester from head to foot the next morning as they worked in the same room, Chester bent over a drawer that tended to stick. "You must have stayed up working on your alphabet."

He nodded, eyes brightening, and held up a finger. He turned the drawer upside down and used his index finger as a pencil to write the letter A, followed by the rest of the alphabet.

Marylu watched his progress with satisfaction. When he got stuck on Q, she spoke the consonant and wrote it on the drawer bottom. Chester tried to imitate her. When he lifted his face, she shook her head. "Remember, the stick goes this way at the end. The other way makes the letter a G."

He tried again, more diligent in his determination than any other person she had ever tried to teach. When he kept writing the stick in the wrong direction, she shifted to stand behind him. She placed her hand over his, her index finger pressing against his to show the direction of the tail of the Q.

His face was inches from hers. A sudden wave of heat gripped her and made her yank her hand away and stand straight. He seemed not to notice her quick retreat. Again he made the circle of the letter and began the line, pausing at the bottom in uncertainty.

Pulling air into her lungs, she leaned forward, doing her best to maintain more distance between them. "Now over to the right and up."

He nodded and finished the letter. He repeated it then went on to finish the alphabet again, but Marylu stopped watching the letters and focused on his hands. His face. The curious little scar over his right eye.

He reminded her of Walter. Not in looks, but in the fact that he was needy. Walter had needed care and the courage to continue what he'd started. He had been near death when Miss Jenny's family had freed him, along with the others. With Marylu's knee strained, and a bone in her ankle broken by the horse, she had determined to keep a vigil by Walter's bed in the hidden room, surrounded by all she needed to care for him through the day. And as their bodies healed, their hearts became knit together.

Likewise, she knew the close proximity to Chester, night after night of teaching him to read and cipher as she planned, would do the same. Over the years of teaching others, she had seen the emotion, almost near worship, that her pupils often lauded her with. In their minds, she had given them a wondrous gift. But despite that, none of the handful of men she had taught had been one she could love, so she had shrugged off their adoration. Chester was a man she could love. Maturity would make her take the path slower than she had with Walter, and with more thought, but first she must choose whether or not to take the path at all. She must not forget the stain of murder was upon him.

When Chester waved a hand in front of her face, she realized she had not only missed his command performance but she'd also been staring at him, lost in her thoughts. Again, she felt the heat rise up her neck and suffuse her cheeks. She took a step back, suddenly confused and afraid.

Chester's soft expression went quizzical and tense. He rose to his feet, a head taller than she. He opened his mouth then closed it.

"I–It's time we be getting back to work." She willed her voice to have some steel. The soft brown orbs stared down at her. Through her. "That drawer's not going to finish sanding itself." A foolish thing to say, and she regretted the rebuke in her tone.

❧

Chester knew fear when he saw it. He saw it in front of him now. Every line of Marylu's face spoke of uncertainty and doubt. Words pushed to his tongue and demanded release, but he could only make noise, so he sought to alleviate her panic with his hands.

Not even her firm rebuke about the drawer deterred him. He advanced on her, and she shrank back a step. He raised his hand slowly and touched hers, the one she held to her cheek. He pulled her hand away, spread his fingers, and pressed it to his chest, where he knew she would feel the strong beat of his heart. His free hand rose to caress her cheek, drawing from courage born of his newfound abilities and the certainty of his feelings.

She did not pull back at his touch. Her eyes slid shut, and her lower lip trembled. He saw the tension rise in her shoulders, and her eyes snapped open, glassy with unshed tears. "I don't even know you. You don't know me."

He let his hand fall away and shrugged his shoulders to transmit his unconcern.

She shook her head, and a single tear spilled down her cheek. She swiped it away and bolted for the door and out of the room, leaving him to stand alone and wonder if the failure had been his for revealing his feelings too soon or hers for allowing whatever dark fear she held to separate her from the courage to love.

Somewhere, somehow, she had been hurt. He was certain of it. And if he hoped to love her, he must prove himself worthy of that love. For the first time in a long time, he thought he might have the courage to do just that.

❧

Marylu avoided the room where Chester worked the rest of the morning. She moved as fast as she could from room to room, complete with her cleaning in record time, except for the room where Chester still sat, the frame of the chest of drawers lying on its side, his dark hands running over the wood in search of rough spots to sand.

She turned from the open doorway, thankful he had not noticed her. She brushed her hand across her brow, the gesture bringing Cooper to mind. She needed to check on him and today, this moment, welcomed the diversion. Anything to take her mind off Chester and the raw emotion that had swelled inside her breast at his touch.

She was too old for love, she decided. Besides, she couldn't get attached to someone who might be a murderer. Marylu pressed a hand to her stomach and wondered, though, what it would be like to love and be loved. To have the children she'd always dreamed of.

She chided herself for such fanciful imaginations. She was Miss Jenny's friend and she could never leave her friend alone.

nine

Chester finished work on the chest of drawers before putting away the tools and sweeping the floor clean of wood dust. In his head, he planned out how to approach making the table Mr. Shillito had asked him to create. He needed more nails to complete the job.

Standing the broom in a corner, he bent to collect the debris, inhaling deeply of the wood dust and shavings, a scent he never tired of. He had worked with wood for years. Even on the plantation, he'd preferred the feel of the warm wood to the labor of picking cotton. His master had seen his skill and taken him from the fields to work with Sam, a boy not much older than his own seventeen years.

Stroking the smooth surface of the completed chairs brought back the good memories of Sam. The days they'd worked together as friends. Before Sam's jealousy had sucked dry the fountain of friendship.

Chester allowed himself the briefest moment to grieve for the bond of brotherhood they had shared. Or he had thought they shared. He should have seen Sam's weakness in the way his friend talked of others, and known it would be the way he would talk about him behind his back. Or even in the way Sam's face had grown dark when the master's wife praised Chester's creations more than Samuel's.

But he hadn't seen it until it was too late and the knife of betrayal had not only stabbed him in the back but also cost him the loss of his tongue.

The euphoria of confidence he'd felt the previous evening crashed. With heavy steps, he crossed to the trash receptacle and dumped the debris. Brushing his hands together, he decided to take a walk. Maybe he'd head over to Hostetter &

Sons' Grocer, where he had first discovered Cooper, to see if the man's cough had cleared up.

He kept his eyes to the ground. Wagons rattled past on the road, and he kept close to the right side. When he shuffled into the town's square, he raised his eyes to the tall clock tower on top of the bank. It touched the underbelly of dark clouds scuttling through the sky.

"You looking for that lazy, no-account Cooper?" Chester raised his eyes to find Cooper's friend, Russell, wrestling a huge crate to the edge of a wagon bed. "I reckon he's at home playing 'possum for Miss Jenny."

Chester arched his brows in question.

"Miss Jenny says to me this morning that he's got himself a cough. She was picking up tea for him. Can you believe that?" Russell steadied the crate, not showing the least discomfort at having several hundred pounds balancing on his shoulder. "Prob'ly got those women waiting on him like he some king."

He might have talked tough, but Chester also saw the worried frown that wiped away the sting of the words. Cooper had told Chester Russell was one of the men on the wagon that night. They'd been good friends for years, and from what Chester had observed that first week of his arrival as Cooper took him around town, the two harped at each other every chance they got.

Chester widened his eyes, then clutched at his chest and pretended to drop over.

The black man hunched down a bit, distributing the weight of the crate onto his back. He chuckled. "Yeah. It'd be just like him to leave on out of this world so's I have to handle these crates by myself."

Chester grinned and waved at the man, his spirit bolstered by Russell's bent toward having fun at Cooper's expense. He followed the train tracks along Carlisle Street, bracketed by residences and businesses that must have had their share of rattling windows and train whistles. He couldn't imagine living so close to such a racket.

He made a left onto Madison, and Miss Jenny's house came into view. It would be good to visit with Cooper. But for all the man's chatter, Chester often sensed a hollowed-out sadness deep down in the man's spirit. Or maybe that was just a reflection of his own sadness.

Chester kept his eyes averted from those along the road, mentally practicing the letters Marylu had taught him. He moved his lips to form each one. His ragged tongue lifted and curled over each letter, though he never tried to give voice, knowing they would be little more than guttural murmurs. Sounds that felt, and sounded, so foreign and ugly.

❧

Marylu hustled west on Baltimore Street toward Greencastle's Square with the intention of checking on Cooper before heading over to help Miss Jenny at the dress shop. She sure needed help. Real bad. Orders were pouring in. No surprise there, what with the wedding season coming up and the variety show over at Town Hall just around the corner.

She murmured greetings to the handful of people lounging in storefronts. At Hostetter & Sons', on the corner of the square, Russell, the grocer's stock boy, talked to a man driving a box wagon. Marylu stopped and backpedaled as Russell raised his hand toward her.

"You tell Cooper he better get himself over here quick. 'Bout near put out my back unloading a shipment from Baltimore this morning."

"I'm going to check on him now. He has himself a nasty cough."

"So I hear." He bent double to lift a small box and waved at the man he'd been talking to. "That Cooper'll get soft with so much attention on him over a cough."

"What you talking about?"

"Miss Jenny was here buying tea for Cooper this morning. Then Chester came by here earlier." He scratched the side of his face against his shoulder. "He went off up Carlisle. Figured he was going to check on him, too."

Marylu squinted up the street as if she would be able to verify Chester's presence right then and there. She debated whether to turn back to the dress shop and leave Cooper in Chester's care. Seemed to her he might not have gone to check on Cooper anyhow. Lots of places and people in town. Who knew where Chester was headed? She better make sure.

Russell was headed toward the doorway of the store but threw a last jibe over his shoulder. "Haven't missed Cooper's talking. Gets me to do the work while he jaws."

Despite his words, she could hear the smile in his voice.

"Tell him I said that, Queenie. It'll put a spring in his step."

Marylu chuckled, embarrassed at his use of her nickname. "I'll tell him you missed him something awful."

Russell set the box down just inside the doorway of the store and popped back out. "You finally meet Chester?"

"Sure did."

"You ask me, I think he's sweet on you."

"Cooper?"

Russell's grin faded. "Him, too, but I was talking 'bout Chester." He hefted another box and headed back toward the store. "Can't talk. Got to get that pile inside before it rains again."

She watched Russell hold the front door open with his foot as he released the box just inside the door then come back out for another one. He remained quiet this time. Dark eyes brooding like a puppy caught in the grain bin. Probably miffed over Cooper being sick and leaving him with the extra work. But, no, that didn't seem right. If there was one thing Russell wasn't afraid of it was work.

She left the man to finish his job and thanked the good Lord again for the special blessing working for Miss Jenny afforded her and Cooper. Some people who had black servants fired them for the least thing, like that Mrs. Burns east of town. But the McGrearys had grown a bond with her mama and daddy. When Miss Jenny came along, she began helping out by keeping an eye on the child. The McGrearys treated her like family, and she and Miss Jenny became fast friends as they grew up together.

When Marylu shoved open the door on Cooper's little house in the McGrearys' backyard, the first thing she smelled was the scent of chicken.

Jenny sat beside Cooper as he sipped from a mug. "That you, Marylu?"

"Sure is. Heard Cooper might be getting too much attention." Cooper grinned and continued to sip. "I see you got some chicken broth down him. Thought you'd be at the store."

"I was going to open up this morning after you left here," Jenny said, "but I was afraid to leave him. I did get out to purchase a tin of tea. . ."

"Heard about it from Russell." Marylu rolled her eyes and motioned to Cooper. "You baby him like he was an infant." She went around to the other side of the bed and pressed her hand against Cooper's forehead. "He still has a fever."

Cooper glared at her and swelled up to cough.

Quick as a wink, she pulled the cup of broth from his hand before the sharp movements of his coughing fit spilled the broth everywhere. She handed the mug to Jenny, eyes still on Cooper. "Reckon we should get to calling the undertaker."

He slid his hand across his mouth and narrowed his eyes at her.

"Honestly." Miss Jenny shook her head.

Marylu turned and motioned for Jenny to follow her outside. She waited while her friend handed the mug back to Cooper and told him to finish it off. When she closed the door behind them, the two huddled, speaking in low tones. Marylu said, "He's still got the fever, and I don't think it'll be gone tonight either."

"I gave him the quinine the doctor left," Jenny said.

"The cough's what worries me most."

"Dr. Kermit didn't seem troubled by it."

"In my experience it's the cough that kills them."

"Marylu!"

"It's the truth."

Jenny drew in a breath and cast a glance toward Cooper's cabin room. "Mrs. Levy is coming in today for those dresses." She turned her blue eyes on Marylu, her tone beseeching. "Stay here with him this afternoon while I tend the shop. He needs someone."

Marylu nodded, touched by the woman's devotion. "I'll do that for you."

"Thank you, Marylu. And there is chicken on the stove—"

"Already seen it and got plans to make a nice pie. You go along and leave things to me."

Miss Jenny tied on her best bonnet, trimmed with a feather that looked more like a bird's wing. "Oh, that reminds me. Chester stopped by about an hour ago."

Her heart pounded harder. "Russell mentioned seeing him."

Jenny's smile widened, and she winked. "I think he was looking for you more than Cooper. I invited him to come back tonight."

ten

The pie dough got too stiff, and Marylu dribbled buttermilk into the bowl to loosen up the lump. Whatever edginess she felt, she took out on the crust as she slapped and dabbed, then rolled and folded. When she finally placed the crust into the pie pan and trimmed it up, she felt better. Something about her conversation with Russell, followed by Jenny's assumption that she was interested in seeing Chester. . . It would be a wonder if the piecrust wasn't ruined by her rough handling.

"You done thumping around in there?"

Marylu brushed her hands together. Clouds of loose flour lifted upward. She smiled. She'd moved him inside where she could get some work done and still keep an eye on him. Seemed to her the patient might be feeling perkier. "You hush your hollering, Cooper, or you won't be getting any of this here chicken potpie."

"Thought you were slaughtering a pig in there. Pie, you—" the last bit got lost as he coughed.

Marylu beat a path to the little room meant for a nursery beside her own. A good spot to hear him holler but far enough away that he could rest. She pulled him upright as he struggled to catch his breath. His body felt cooler. Something to be grateful for, but she still didn't like that cough.

When Cooper finally quieted, she lit into him. "What you doin' hollering at me through the walls? You need to stay still and shut your mouth, or you'll give yourself another fit." She lowered him to the bed and pressed her hand to his face. "Least your fever seems to have broke."

"How long I been sleeping?" he asked.

"Long enough for me to clean this here house from cellar

to attic." She didn't like the way the coughing fit seemed to drain him or how he looked so thin and frail.

"Gotta get up." Again the cough seized him.

Marylu placed her hand on his shoulder. "You'll do nothing of the sort. Rest."

His gaze locked on her, and he raised his hand as if to touch her cheek. For a fleeting moment, she thought she saw something soft in his eyes. But the next second his hand fell away and his eyes shut. His breathing evened out.

Not used to his going quiet so suddenly, Marylu steeled herself not to panic. She reached out and touched his cheek. Fear gripped her hard as she imagined the grim possibility that Cooper might not make it through this sickness. She'd miss him. Sorely miss him. Miss Jenny, too, would grieve mightily over the loss.

Marylu got to her feet and stretched her back. She needed to set the kettle to singing and put together some tea. She made short work of filling the crust with chunks of chicken, carrots, and potatoes and covering it with another crust. Tea steeped in a mug for Cooper, and she crushed a clove of garlic to spin around in the amber liquid and hopefully take the edge off that cough. As the garlic steeped, she got down the Bible and set it in its place of honor. If Chester got here soon enough, he could read with them.

Miss Jenny chose that moment to open the door.

Marylu formed the words of a cheery greeting as she turned that direction, but the sight of tears streaking her friend's cheeks froze Marylu's feet flat to the floor and her tongue to the roof of her mouth.

Jenny sniffed and forced a smile as she untied her bonnet and removed it. "I expect I look a sight."

"You look like someone sat on your prettiest bonnet."

"I'm being silly." Jenny brushed at her cheeks and smoothed a hand down the front of her dress. "That pie smells wonderful. And tea's ready! Thank you so much."

Marylu wasn't fooled. "You done gushing? You know I

always have tea waiting for you, and that pie hasn't even gotten hot yet."

Jenny sighed and Marylu wasted no time in crossing the room and bringing her friend into the circle of her arms. "You tell Marylu what's got you crying."

For a minute she wondered if Jenny would reply. She didn't let go, forcing the woman to relax in her embrace. Marylu had held Jenny McGreary and calmed her tears and fears since the first time she'd scraped her knee on a nail and thought she was gonna bleed to death.

Finally, Jenny rested her head on Marylu's shoulder and released a sigh. "Sally Worth came into the store."

Marylu pulled back but maintained a hold on Jenny's upper arms. "What's she doing in there? She always gets her dresses done over at—" Marylu sucked in a breath. It made sense. And knowing Sally the way she did. . . "She's wanting you to make her a dress for some special occasion she's sharing with Aaron Walck."

It was Jenny's turn to gasp. "How could you have known that?"

Marylu whirled away. "It's just the kind of person she is. She wouldn't come to McGreary's Dress Shop unless it was to gloat about some bit of favor she'd gained with Mr. Walck." As she poured tea into a cup for Miss Jenny, another thing became certain that she had only suspected before. She set the steaming cup in front of her friend. "You really care for him." Sure she had known Miss Jenny thought the man's plight a sad thing, that she felt deeply for the ache of his loss. His late wife had been one of Jenny's favorite customers.

The love between the Walcks had been witnessed by the entire town. Just as the sorrow in Aaron's eyes when she died had been witnessed. Marylu especially recalled his lost look as his wife's coffin had been lowered into the saturated ground, rain pouring down on the crowd of mourners. Jenny had seemed mesmerized that day by the sight of Aaron's hair plastered to his head, his coat dripping wet. The palpable grief. Even as others filed away, he had stayed. Dazed. Probably afraid to leave the gaping hole in the ground. It had taken Marylu a full five minutes to coax Jenny away from the graveside and out of the rain.

Lord, this child's tender heart deserves to be loved by a man who can love that hard.

&

Chester bounded up the back step, figuring someone inside would know why his knock on Cooper's cabin door went unanswered. Surely the man hadn't recovered that quick.

He smoothed his newly clipped hair down, pleased with the ease with which he could manage it now, and raised his hand to knock. He heard muffled voices and the sound of steps before the door swung inward to reveal Jenny McGreary. Chester's excitement dwindled a bit, but he nodded at the woman and lowered his gaze. Scents of home cooking with undertones of spice swirled in the air, and he breathed deeply.

"Please, won't you come in, Chester?"

He raised his head and caught Miss Jenny's smile. He did his best to keep his eyes somewhere other than her face, but when she placed her hand along his arm and tugged him inside, he couldn't help but gape up into her blue eyes.

She gave him a soft smile and held up a finger to let him know to wait. She hesitated, looking embarrassed, then laughed. "I forget you can hear just fine. Right?"

Chester nodded.

"Marylu's quite the cook. Would you like something to eat?"

Chester shook his head and set his slate and pencil on the table. He would never be able to reconcile himself to the idea of a white woman serving him.

Marylu burst into the room just then. She paused in the doorway to wipe her hands on her apron.

He basked in her smile and the way it spilled sunshine into the cold corners of his spirit.

"Sure he wants something to eat. You ever known a single man to turn down cookin' that ain't his own?"

Miss Jenny chuckled and scooted out the bench across from him. She settled her skirts around her and sat down. Marylu made for the stove as Miss Jenny slid the Bible closer and opened it up.

The women chatted a bit about their days, and Chester listened, content to be in the home and in Marylu's presence. Before he knew it, she wielded a huge spoon over a hot dish and slipped something with a golden crust and the smell of heaven right in front of him. His stomach rumbled so loudly that Miss Jenny sent him a soft smile. He felt the heat flush into his cheeks and bowed his head.

"Now eat up," Marylu said. "I'm going to take this broth to Cooper."

Chester shook his head and pointed toward the back door. He pantomimed knocking on Cooper's door, then shrugged and shook his head.

Marylu beamed sunshine down on him. "You're right in that. I brought him inside to keep a good eye on him and so I could get some things done."

Chester nodded and picked up his fork. He stole a glance at Miss Jenny. She winked at him and bowed her head. The blessing was short, and the whole idea of his sitting across from her and eating a supper seemed a strange dream that left him feeling both uneasy and confident. She seemed in a world of her own as she worked a carrot onto her fork, and Chester contented himself with cutting his chicken into smaller pieces with the side of his fork. Little bites he could manage, though the whole process of eating took him time.

Through the open doorway he could hear Marylu's voice but could not make out what she was saying to Cooper. The old man's responses were punctuated with deep coughs that even pulled Miss Jenny up straight.

Her worried eyes focused on Chester.

When he caught the worry in Miss Jenny's eyes, he set his fork aside and clasped his hands together to indicate she should pray. His aunt had coughed like that right before she died, two years before he'd left to make his own way.

"Yes, I have. It's just so much easier to worry than to pray." A sigh escaped her lips. "Do you believe, Chester?"

The question took him by surprise. His mother had believed, her rich alto caressing the words of the old hymns she used to sing in the late evening after hours of washing laundry or spent tending the garden, or the hundred other tasks of day-to-day living. His father loved to hear his mother's voice, but he never joined in, and Chester often suspected that somewhere along the line his father's belief had been snuffed out.

Where did that leave him? Did he believe in God? Of course. He never once doubted an omniscient Spirit who created the world and everything in it. But he knew Miss Jenny's question went deeper than that, and he didn't know how to respond. At one time he'd been a good man who tried to respect his mama's God, but Sam's betrayal had shaken him. Watching the master fall, witnessing the blood. . . It had been too easy to hate since that moment.

His hesitation must have answered the unspoken question, but Chester shrugged and pointed to his heart then to the Bible.

"Would you like me to read it to you?"

To read. Wasn't that the world Marylu had promised to open to him by teaching him letters? And now a white woman was willing to read to him?

Marylu bustled back into the room. "That man is the most ornery critter I've ever encountered." She stopped and shot him a glance. "Make that the second orneriest critter I've encountered."

Chester's grin was huge.

"I was getting ready to read the Bible, Marylu. Will you join us?"

"I'm thinking we need to go in to the room with Cooper. Read something about hard hearts or that talking donkey of that Beulah fellow."

"Balaam."

eleven

Truth be told, Marylu had never felt like she felt sitting next to Chester and watching him drink in every letter and vowel. His quick mind pleased her greatly. Yet she wanted to hear him speak. If he never tried, did that mean he couldn't?

As he bowed his head over the slate and worked on a couple of simple words, she went over the alphabet in her mind, paying close attention to how her tongue curled and worked around every letter. If she could teach him how to use what was left of his tongue, it just might work.

When he lifted his head, she inhaled a deep breath. "Let's work on your speech."

Chester flinched.

"It can be done. Some letters you'll have a harder time with, but the rest you'll catch on to quick-like."

He nodded slowly, and she saw the smear of disbelief tighten his forehead.

She reached out and touched his fingers. "We can do it. Together."

His eyes fell to the place where her fingers covered his. She followed his gaze. Beneath hers, the squareness of his hands dwarfed her own. She imagined the power in those hands from all the sanding and hammering, and she wondered, too, if the pads of his fingers would be rough from working with wood or smooth and. . . She snatched her hand away and cleared her throat. "Best we get started."

Chester's eyes searched hers, and she saw a challenge there. Yet she hardly knew this man and had no right to feel anything other than friendship. Not this soon. He'd come to town, the label of "murderer" hard on his heels, and other than working for Mr. Shillito and knowing Cooper, fixing

61

him some food and cutting his hair, what did she know of him?

Sure, he stirred things in her that had lain dormant since Walter, but circumstances were different now. She had changed. Matured. And she would not give her heart away so easily. Weariness settled over her shoulders. It seemed she often chided herself with the same argument, when it would be so much easier to simply allow the feelings Chester stirred in her heart.

Marylu steeled herself and stared at a point over his shoulder. She said the letter A, then formed it with her tongue in a melodramatic way that allowed him to see how her tongue moved. He tried to imitate. The sound was garbled, but she made him try again, over and over. They worked through the first six letters.

He concentrated hard and worked even harder, doing his best to follow her directions. Seeing his torn tongue made her heart sad, and several times it came to her mind to ask him about the incident. About the rumor that he had murdered. But to watch the fervor with which he worked to regain his speech and to learn to read, she reasoned it had to be the idle talk of a bored woman. Mrs. Burns's reputation as a gossip preceded her. And Chester had no way of defending himself against rumors, whether true or not. One day, when he could communicate better, she would ask him about it. At the quick rate with which he picked up on the alphabet and the few small words, she would not have to wait long.

The arguments, for and against Chester, ran through her head as they worked together over the next hour. And new things were added to the list of sensations and tenderness his presence stirred.

The flicker of the lantern light against his skin, smooth and dark like leather.

The way his eyes squinted when he concentrated.

And when he raised his eyes to hers after a particular triumph, the warm glow in the depths of his maple syrup gaze spilled over her like warm honey.

When they took a break from speech and went back to writing, he couldn't seem to remember the right way to hold the pencil. She demonstrated a new way. When he couldn't quite get his fingers into the right position, she took his hand in hers and curled his long fingers around the instrument, suspecting all along that his forgetfulness had little to do with his mind and everything to do with her touch. And she played along. On those occasions when their eyes did meet, she tried to cover what his gaze stirred by concentrating on the slate or ignoring him, but she couldn't deny it to herself.

№

Evening after evening, for an entire week, they worked, and when she walked into McGreary's dress shop that bright Friday morning and saw Mrs. Burns standing in front of the mirror for a fitting, Marylu made up her mind to draw out the woman more on the accusation against Chester.

№

Jenny stood with a mouthful of pins, as was usual for her during a fitting. It came to Marylu in that moment that she would have to do very little to coax Mrs. Burns to speak up about Chester. So she sidled up next to Jenny and prepared to get down on the floor to pin the hem.

Jenny stopped her and took the pins from her mouth. "I'm having trouble on that dress." Jenny jerked her head to indicate the table behind her.

Marylu noticed the striped material of Sally Worth's gown. The one she'd come in to the shop to have Jenny make so she could brag about her "date" with Aaron Walck. As Marylu ran her fingers over the material, she saw the ripped threads, evidence of Jenny's frustration. Probably less over the gown than over the owner.

If Jenny didn't want to mess with the sewing of Sally's dress, she would certainly take over. Anything to help her friend bear the disappointment of Aaron's choice. She took a seat and threaded her needle. The first poke through the striped silk coincided with Mrs. Burns's first question.

"I heard you were helping that deaf boy learn to spell, Marylu. Is it true?"

Behind the woman's back, Marylu raised her eyes from the dress, straight up to the heavens. And grinned.

Jenny jumped in to answer before Marylu could give voice. "She has, Mrs. Burns. Chester's not deaf at all, just unable to express himself very well."

"Yes, I know. He got his tongue cut out for murdering his master. Heard the story from one of our servants."

By "servant," Marylu knew Mrs. Burns meant Gladys, their black house servant. Gladys's tongue was as well-oiled as Mrs. Burns.

"He's a gentle soul that needs attention." Marylu took a stab at the material with her needle. "He's smarter than most and knows how to still his tongue quite nicely. It's one thing I greatly admire in a body."

Jenny cleared her throat and tugged down on the bodice of the dress Mrs. Burns modeled. She released a stream of chatter meant to distract her client from the implication of Marylu's words.

But the burn of the woman's audacity singed along Marylu's arms and feet. She bent her head over her work and prayed God would help her not to break a commandment.

Marylu grunted a silent "amen" to her prayer just as the door to the shop opened again. Sally Worth glided in, and Marylu started praying all over again. She watched as Jenny turned to see who had entered the shop and applauded her friend for not allowing a trace of emotion to give away her true feelings on her rival's presence. Instead, Marylu felt the pain for Jenny. The memory of her tears the week before turned her heart inside out all over again.

She dug her needle deeper into the material and brought the needlework closer to her face. If she buried herself in her work, maybe she could drown out the conversation that she knew, deep in her bones, was coming. Sally would shoot off about something regarding Aaron, trying to get Jenny jealous. Or in tears.

Her hands tightened on the fabric. *Lord, have mercy on my soul. Help the law of kindness to be in my tongue.*

Mrs. Burns and Sally chatted amicably as Jenny, still with pins in her mouth, continued along the hem of the unfinished gown. If not for Miss Jenny being in the middle of the thing, Marylu would have heaved herself right out of the chair and gone out back until everyone left the store, but she had to stay. Had to protect her employer from the barbs that were sure to fly and be a tongue for her friend, since Jenny's mouth was full.

"Well, *Miss* McGreary," Sally's strident voice dripped, "why, you must get so filthy down on that floor all day long. How do you manage to get the stains out of your skirts?"

And here we go. . . Marylu huffed and stared up at Sally's wide-eyed innocence.

Jenny did her best to smile around the pins in her mouth.

"You work so hard," Sally continued.

Mrs. Burns smoothed a hand down the fabric of her gown. "But she does create some lovely things."

Marylu silently patted Mrs. Burns on the back for that bit of niceness.

Jenny rose to her feet in a smooth motion and removed the pins from her lips. "There you go, Mrs. Burns. I'll have everything done by Monday. Would that suit you?"

"That is just fine." The elder woman swished around in her finery a minute then headed to the back room.

Jenny followed the woman.

Marylu kept a sharp eye on Sally, as that one made her way ever closer to the place where Marylu sat working her needle. "I'll be so excited to wear this to the show."

Marylu chose to take the high road. "Yes, Mrs. Burns is correct in that Miss McGreary does fine work. You'll hold your head high wearing this frock."

"Oh, Marylu. I'm not used to servants speaking first." Sally gave a little laugh. "I forget how Jenny coddles you and

Cooper." She laced her fingers and a little smile bloomed on her lips. But it wasn't a nice smile. "It won't be the dress so much as the man with me. Mr. Walck is most handsome."

A grunt crawled up her throat, but Marylu squelched it before it squeezed out. Miss Sally would think it most unladylike of her. Not that Marylu regarded herself as a lady, but a woman, of course. Even if regarded by others as a servant who happened to have black skin.

"I know how much his attentions mean to Miss McGreary. It must pain her deeply to watch his attention shift to me."

Marylu took another hard stab at the material and poured out every prayer for grace she could think of. Let the woman blather on about her catch. If Aaron Walck thought Sally Worth worth his time, then he wasn't the one for Jenny.

"The material is so soft and so beautiful and so expensive," she purred. "But daddy told me to get what I wanted."

Marylu had no idea why Sally's daddy would be so keen on his daughter marrying a widower, versus one of the other nice and never-married young men in town. Unless it meant money.

"Daddy thinks his business, combined with Aaron's, could be very prosperous."

Marylu hid the small smile that twitched at her lips. Let people talk long enough and they'll answer all the questions for you.

Sally tapped her foot, and Marylu imagined the woman was getting tired of carrying on a one-sided conversation. "Jenny said the dress would be done this afternoon."

She raised her eyes to the young woman. "Done so that you can try it on but not done for you to take home. Miss McGreary'll want to fit you before finishing the dress." She lowered her eyes again. "I'll be finished basting it up in about fifteen minutes."

The sound of voices carried from the back. Mrs. Burns and Jenny made their way into the room. "I'll send Teddy over to pick up the gowns tomorrow morning."

"That would be fine, Mrs. Burns."

Without further conversation, but a nod to Sally, the elder woman glided toward the door and pulled it open.

Tension seemed to build as Miss Jenny turned to face Sally. The smile on her friend's face flattened at the corners and proved, at least to Marylu, how stressful Sally's presence was.

"I hope Marylu has helped you, Miss Worth."

Marylu watched Sally swell up for her response. Something caught Marylu's eye at the front of the store, where the door never had shut upon Mrs. Burns's exit. Instead, another person entered, tall and handsome. As Sally's voice raised in irritation at Jenny, Marylu nodded to Aaron Walck. He returned the greeting almost absently, his attention hooked on Sally and Jenny and the tirade falling from Sally's lips.

"And it's not even done yet! I've got a busy schedule, and now I'll have to wait until tomorrow. I wanted to wear it to the minstrel show at Town Hall. You better hope it gives me enough time to find new shoes!"

Jenny gave Marylu a sideways glance.

Marylu signaled with her eyes at the tall form standing just inside the door, even as she responded to Sally's words. "Told her I'd be done with the basting in fifteen minutes."

When Jenny caught sight of the newcomer, she gasped.

Sally turned. "Aaron! Did you get what you needed at the hardware store?"

Marylu's stomach soured at the hypocrisy of the woman.

Jenny's expression showed nothing. "If you could wait, Miss Worth, I'm sure Marylu will be as good as her word and have the dress basted for a fitting." There were equal parts steel and politeness in Jenny's voice.

Sally sashayed over to Aaron and took his arm. "We were just talking about my dress for the variety show. Want to see it?"

Aaron stared down at Sally for a full minute before allowing himself to be drawn closer to the spot where Marylu worked over the fabric. She didn't see one bit of warmth in the man's demeanor and hoped that witnessing

Sally's tirade might help him realize his mistake.

"As I said," Sally's voice held a forced edge of gentleness as she finally replied to Jenny's suggestion, "I can't wait. Aaron is taking me on a picnic." She gazed up at him with more heat than Marylu thought fitting.

Aaron grimaced. "About that. . ." He fidgeted. "I won't be able to this afternoon. One of the tools I'd ordered came in, and Edgar's man is delivering it this afternoon."

Sally stiffened and drew away from him. She seemed at a loss for words.

Jenny took the chance the silence offered her. "Then you can stay and wait for the dress."

"No," Sally spit out. "I won't be staying. Perhaps I'll just cancel my order if you're not able to keep your end of the bargain."

"That's fine," Jenny allowed.

Sally's chin jutted. "Fine." She hooked her arm back through Aaron's. "Consider my order canceled."

Aaron's eyes darted between Marylu and Jenny, finally settling on Jenny. He looked sorrier than sorry to Marylu's mind but allowed himself to be wheeled around and tugged toward the front door. He held it open as Sally made her exit and sent one last pained look toward Jenny.

As soon as the door shut behind them, Marylu lumbered upward and gathered her friend into her arms. Words of praise died when she felt Jenny's shoulders sag and heard the sharp intake of breath that indicated tears.

twelve

Cooper's recovery was slow. Between Marylu, Miss Jenny, and Chester, they took turns checking on him during the day and through the night.

Marylu and Chester worked on his words and speech. He became even more pleased with his progress when Marylu and Jenny could understand his talking, even if the words were simple and the letters not the ones that gave him trouble.

His presence in the home simultaneously gave him a sense of family and smote him for not getting over to Mercersburg to see his mother and sister. But his hesitation, he realized, stemmed more than anything from his desire to return to his mama whole. Or as whole as he could be with only half his tongue. He wanted her to be proud of the man he had become, but he feared the rumors of his master's death had reached her ears. She would be able to look at him and know he had suffered for it. She would understand how far and how long he had run to escape, not only those who searched for him to kill him for the deed but also the specter of his own failure at being a man of worth.

The failure ate at him. As he entered Cooper's cabin, Chester clutched what was in his pocket and forced his mind to review the instructions Marylu had given him that morning. "Make sure he drinks his tea. And give him some firm slaps on the back to dislodge the mucus in his chest." It was the same thing she'd told him for the last three days.

Chester slipped over to the bed, satisfied to see the man sleeping. He turned to leave when Cooper's voice caught him. "If'n I'm awake, you promise not to force me to swallow that tea Marylu's been having you make?"

Chester grinned, noting that Cooper's voice seemed less hoarse than it had in the past week.

"You're a good friend keeping up with me, Chester." Cooper wiggled himself upright in bed. "Marylu's forced enough of her herbal teas down my throat to heal a tribe of Indians."

Chester nodded. He produced the tin of loose tea he'd bought at Hostetter & Sons' Grocer and held it up for Cooper to see.

The old man groaned. "If the cough don't put me six feet under, the tea sure enough will. You know she makes me drink it with garlic?" Cooper shook his head. "She's something else, that's for sure."

Somehow it didn't seem right to simply smile a response and act like he hadn't noticed Cooper's preoccupation with Marylu. At first he had taken Cooper's flapping over Marylu's care for him as a man not enjoying being sick. Understandable. But then he realized that the old man's griping was more to mask other things. Deeper feelings. Chester had seen it in the way Cooper's rheumy eyes followed her every move, and though his mouth got saucy right back at Marylu, it was those times Chester caught him watching her that spoke the truth.

Chester heaved a sigh and raised his hands. He pointed at Cooper then to his chest to indicate his heart.

Cooper shook his head. "Don't start all that. Talk."

He worked up the courage to say what he'd been about to mime, and the words flew out of his mouth, rough and awkward. "You love Marylu."

The old man blinked and stared. His eyes sharpened and flashed, then he dropped his gaze to his hands, gnarled together in his lap. "She's a good woman. Always been the kind I'd wished I'd settled down with, but she'd never have a man like me. Too old for her anyway. I've always known that."

"She care for you." Chester formed the words with some difficulty.

Cooper paused, obviously taking the time to figure out what Chester had said. He reached behind him and punched the pillow. "It don't matter now anyway. I'm too old." Cooper's gaze went sharp and clear and pierced Chester through. "But not you. She could love you."

Chester opened his mouth to form a protest.

"You need a woman like her."

The statement hung between them. Chester shifted his weight and held up the tin as an excuse to leave.

As he dipped water from the dipping box outside Jenny's kitchen, he warred with himself on what to say to Cooper. On how to act. While he had been picking up on Cooper's affection for Marylu, it seemed Cooper had recognized Chester's feelings for her as well. Yet he knew he could never be worthy of her. He had nothing to offer.

But Cooper's words bolstered him, too. If anyone knew Marylu, it would be him. Perhaps the old man thought Marylu might welcome Chester's love, else why would he suggest such a thing?

The whole exchange gnawed at Chester. Long past his visit with Cooper and into the night when he sat next to Marylu and worked on his words and speech, the conversation drummed a positive beat against the negatives. Every time their hands brushed, his senses sparked. He wondered if she felt it, too, and explored her features, her eyes, for any sign of what she felt.

She demonstrated how her tongue formed the letter L, and he concentrated harder. He found the letter particularly frustrating and worked his tongue over and over to get the flow of it. When the sound rumbled up from his chest, his tongue seemed too weak to carry off the rolling sound and it became the letter W. He tried again and again.

Marylu finally shook her head. "Let's let it rest for now. It's coming out better, but we've got other things to work on."

He picked up the slate and began writing words. When he finished cramming the entire surface with most of what he'd learned, he held it up. The pleased expression on her face brought a wave of satisfaction. And when she didn't look away, something changed. Her gaze became searching. Questioning. Fear etched a mark between her brows.

Chester's heart seemed to slow its rhythm then speed up. He felt a million things in a matter of seconds. And he felt nothing at all. Her eyes reminded him of the dark grain of the walnut wood he used to build his master's bookcases down in the South. He lifted his hand to grab the rag and erase the slate but stopped.

Her hand rested on the table, and he lowered his to hers, slowly, afraid his intentions would bleed through her mind and she would snatch away. Her skin was soft, and she glanced down at their hands with an expression of wonder. He inhaled and could smell the freshness of lye soap mixed with the chicken she'd fried for their meal.

In the hotel room, all those weeks ago, she had seemed panicked by his touch. Even through their evenings together, as his own feelings had built, he had wondered about that moment and what it was that held her aloof from him.

But now, here, this moment, she seemed soft, her eyes showing a gentleness way down deep. For him. He squeezed her hand and smiled.

She always seemed so brave and strong. Sure of herself in a way he'd never been. Her strength drew him, and he wondered if what he felt with her could possibly be the elusive thing he'd longed for all his life.

He breathed deeper, easier breaths, and an urgency to give voice to his feelings rose in him, buoyed by Cooper's observation.

"You need a woman like her."

"I love you." The L didn't come out right at all, but she understood. He could see it in the widening of her eyes and the way her lips parted. He gloried in her expression, the effect of his words, and he never felt anything harder than he did the satisfaction of having those feelings spoken out loud.

❧

Marylu felt every inch the woman caught in a summertime thunderstorm. This one assaulted her, not with water but with a deluge of emotion that rolled her over and over.

Chester's face mapped out the wrinkles of a hard life, but his eyes glowed with hope.

Time stood still. Her breath caught. He loved her. The wonder of the words rolled and spun and skipped through her heart. His warm hand squeezed hers, and the words slipped over her tongue, poised and waiting to be released.

Her gaze fell to the slate between them and all the words crowded there. She was transported back in time to Walter's slate, filled with words. The quick brush of his lips after he had praised her for being such a good teacher.

The shock of memory jolted Marylu, and she suddenly understood the burst of emotion that had caused Chester to utter such a precious phrase.

How easy it had been for Walter to love her when he saw her not as a man should see a woman but as a pupil feels appreciation and tenderness for a teacher. She had seen it in the handful of men she had taught over the years since Walter. Then there was always the hard reality—true love would never have allowed Walter to leave her side, but infatuation was fickle and slippery.

And now another pupil declared his love.

And she had this minute to respond.

No words came. At the point where communication became essential, her tongue, healthy and whole, failed. And the specter of her doubts charged to the fore of her thinking. What she felt for him gripped her hard. Still, even after weeks together, she hardly knew him. With his newfound ability to talk, she could now ask him the question that burned through her every time she felt the softer emotions swirl in her heart. She was afraid to hear his answer, for should it be affirmative, she would be crushed. She could never love a man whose moral character she could not condone. She valued life too much.

The question begged to be asked. So simple to give voice and finally put to rest her own doubts. Simple, yes, but staring into his eyes, so hopeful and vulnerable, made her ashamed to believe the flapping tongue of Mrs. Burns over a man whose sincerity she had witnessed time and again. But she had to ask.

"There is a rumor," she said, her voice low and intense, "that you murdered someone."

His expression shifted ever so slightly. Surprise mingled with something else, and his gaze skittered to the surface of the table.

She closed her eyes and swallowed, recognizing what his averted gaze meant. Not the innocence she had hoped for, but resignation. Even fear.

thirteen

Chester clutched the slate that Marylu had placed in his hands right before she opened the door for him to leave. Her question hovered, unanswered, between them. An effective barrier that he didn't know how to cross.

He chided himself for not trying and, instead, allowing Sam's betrayal to win, again, his silence. But Marylu's question had so taken him off-guard. In his head, the words of his defense formed. He could explain the situation in detail, but only with great care would he be able to say the words out loud. Dredging up his past. Reliving the chase. The dogs. Loneliness. Days of hunger followed by nights of cold that froze his bones. The explanation itself proved an obstruction, insurmountable. Yet his silence won him nothing.

He wandered through the night, without thought of where he was or what he wanted to do. Mind blank. Body riddled with hurt and embarrassment and a hundred other painful feelings.

When the terrible shock faded, he thought of heading out to Mercersburg. He could stay with his mama and siblings. Find work. No one in Greencastle would miss him, except Mr. Shillito, but replacing him would not be a problem.

Exhaustion weighted his steps. Finally, he tripped and fell. He lay there, wanting to never get up. Instead, he rolled onto his back. Blackness obscured everything, the moon hanging behind a cloud. Walking in the dark, ten miles to Mercersburg, seemed too daunting a task. But he wanted to go. Needed to run just as he had needed to when his master's head hit that boulder.

Samuel's voice rang in his head. *"Better run hard and fast and hope no one ever catches you for killing the master."*

He got to his feet slowly, straightening with effort, and squinted into the dimness. His path had led him through town and along a vast field of trees lined like soldiers. An orchard. Behind him lay the outline of the town's buildings, and he did an about-face. As he placed one foot in front of another, he laid his plans for leaving. He would rest through the night, talk to Mr. Shillito in the morning, then begin the trek to Mercersburg. Seeing his mother and brothers and sisters again. . . Excitement coiled in his stomach and leaked into his limbs, until he walked at a pace that left him breathless.

Antrim House came into view and he slowed, grateful for his room. He would ask Mr. Shillito if he knew someone in Mercersburg who needed a hired hand and even prayed the man might. It would save him time looking for a job.

A shadow moved in front of Chester. His heart slammed hard, and he tensed. When the form shifted again, Chester relaxed. He recognized the slender outline of Zedikiah. For the last week, Zedikiah had sought him out more and more, even sleeping on the floor in his room two nights in a row, but only one of those nights had he been drunk. The smell of alcohol grew stronger as Chester neared the swaying form. He reached out to touch the boy.

Zedikiah tensed.

"Chester." He said his name to ease the boy's tension.

"I'm sick," Zedikiah whined.

Chester wedged his shoulder underneath the boy's and reached to push open the door to the hotel. Zedikiah stumbled through the doorway under his own steam, and Chester shut the door to the hotel then swung open the door to his room. The boy lurched inside, staggered, and fell into a heap. He lay there, sprawled, not caring, already breathing heavily.

Chester sat down on the edge of his bed and stared at the still form. He had talked with Zedikiah about his woodworking, even showed him a couple of tricks he had learned, but in all his days here in Greencastle, he had never addressed the boy's drinking problem.

He knew little of Zedikiah's past, except that his mama had been dead for a year. Clearly, with no one to guide him, the boy had lost his way.

How well he understood.

Except Chester's mama hadn't died. He had left her, and all he had known, because stubbornness drove him to leave and foolhardy imagination told him he would be able to make it. Those lonely days in the South, when he'd first been captured and sold to a huge plantation in the middle of a country foreign to him, he had known a despair so deep and cutting that he had been lured to taste alcohol. Its numbing qualities eased the hurt, but the aftermath of his binges made the drinking a vile thing. Only, the ache of loneliness that plagued him outstripped the vileness, and he had continued to imbibe.

His cure came in the form of a whipping, when one morning the drinking caused him to be late to the fields. The master's son had administered the "cure" by laying his back bare with the whip. The young woman who tended his wounds invited him to go with her and the other slaves to the little church down the road. So, on Sundays, with the rest of his ragtag slave family, he began attending with Lily, the young woman. His soul awakened to the comfort he recalled his mother talking about. And he came to believe that his mama's Lord would help him.

And now, he had a young boy falling prey to the same siren song of drink. Zedikiah's presence here, tonight, meant he trusted Chester, but it would take more than trust to help the boy. Zedikiah needed love and support and courage.

"Zedikiah." His tongue tripped over the Z. He clenched his fists and tried the boy's name again. He couldn't make his tongue feel the letter and, instead, knelt to shake the boy awake.

Zedikiah's body twitched and his eyes opened briefly, unfocused.

Chester pulled him upward and wedged his shoulder underneath to pull him to a sitting position. "Wake up," he commanded.

His strength didn't match the dead weight of the young man, though, and Zedikiah fell back again. A moan slipped from his lips, and he rolled away and curled into a ball, as if hurt.

Chester frowned at the inert form and yanked the blanket off his bed. He shook it and let it float downward to cover the boy. He stretched out on the mattress, willing sleep to come, half praying, half begging God to send the burden of helping Zedikiah to someone else. After all, he needed to leave town.

&

Guilt burned through Marylu's mind after Chester left. By turns, she chided herself for asking the question and him for not answering. He should understand her need to know the truth. Even if he couldn't talk well, he surely knew she was patient enough to listen as he talked or wrote it out.

She paced and prayed and fretted and grew angrier by the minute. It was too soon for him to tell her he loved her. They weren't youths in the throes of romantic notions. At least she wasn't, nor would she allow herself to be. They were two mature individuals who had seen clearly how love didn't always conquer. And her teaching him to write and read and talk didn't make her a hero. It made her a woman who cared and wanted to help.

There was no fool way she would love a man so quickly again. Not after Walter. There were things about Chester she sure liked, times he made her feel that same giddiness she had felt over Walter, but it had been infatuation then and must also be infatuation now.

"What the world you doing in there?" Cooper's voice broke her reverie.

Marylu pivoted. A board creaked. "You hush and go back to sleep. You'll wake Miss Jenny with your hollering." Not that she, herself, wasn't doing a good job of it.

The telltale shuffle of Cooper's footsteps let her know he was headed her way. She sighed and sat down on the bench at the table.

"I heard that board creak a thousand times." Cooper popped through the doorway and stared hard at her. "Thought I was having a dream until I realized it was you making the racket." He looked around the room, eyebrows arched. "Where's Chester? Thought he'd still be here working on his talking."

"He left."

Cooper's gaze landed on her, searching. "Something happen I should be knowing about?"

How she wished Miss Jenny had been the one to come down the stairs. No use shedding water on the table in front of Cooper. He'd curl into a ball of agony if she sprung a leak.

"Marylu?"

If there was ever a serious bone in Cooper's body, he showed it in the soft question that was her name. His tenderness caught at her, and she waved him into the room. "I'll get you something."

"Just stay put." He pushed away from the door frame and crossed to the chair. "You always fuss over me like I'm some old man that can't do a thing for myself."

"You can't."

"Can too and you know it. And the last thing I want is a cup of your tea. Whoever put garlic in tea anyway?"

"It's good for you. Gives you spunk, and you sure were needing it."

"It gives me bad breath."

"You already had that."

Cooper chuckled and shook his head. "Chester tell you he's sweet on you or some such foolishness?"

The sudden change in conversation brought her up sharp. She narrowed her eyes. "He been talking to you about me?"

"Thinks you're a fine woman."

"I don't hold to you two talking about me behind my back."

Cooper didn't back down. "You think women have a corner on that market? Not gossip talk." He shook his head. "Man-to-man talk."

"Ain't you one man short?"

Cooper snorted. "That's no way to talk about Chester." He cocked his head and stabbed a finger at her. "Now what's got you riled up?"

She wanted to duck that direct question. Her skin burned with the shame of what she'd done. Whether she needed the reassurance or not, her timing for asking the question of Chester couldn't have been worse, and she knew Cooper would tell her so.

"Must be bad if you can't be looking me in the eyes."

Marylu did her best not to break down right there, and so, for the first time in a long time, she dared to tell him exactly what she thought. "Not bad." She pulled in a long, slow breath. "I just wanted to know about the rumor of him murdering someone."

Cooper pursed his lips. "Yup."

She tilted a look at him. "What you mean, 'Yup?'"

"He sure did do something. If you wanted to know, you should have asked me."

"Mrs. Burns said that he killed his master, but I should be able to ask him."

"Well you asked him. Why'd he leave?"

She didn't know. Not really. Why did he leave? Shame? Fear?

Cooper sat up straight, his eyes grave. "Got the story from another black who jumped off the train with Chester. Recognized him from years before. What I got from him was that Chester's friend made it look like he'd stolen from the master. When the master went to punish Chester for the deed by laying stripes along his back then cutting out his tongue for lying about it, Chester, struggling for his freedom, pushed the man, and he slammed his head a good one on a pile of rocks removed from the fields. Broke his neck or something.

Master's son chased him with dogs and posted an ad to get him returned, but no one never caught him."

Relief streamed through Marylu's body. Then guilt pinched along her spine. And anger. Why hadn't he just told her?

"You've got poison in your eyes." Cooper raised his brows and rubbed his jaw.

She leveled her gaze on Cooper. Chester had fought back against an unfair deed. She'd known something haunted him. In all her days helping the McGrearys run the "station" on the Underground Railroad, she had heard many stories, but, though compassionate, the cruelty had never quite touched her. Perhaps it had been her youthful naiveté. Walter often told her how good she had it with Miss Jenny's family, and though Russell and many of those who had stayed in Greencastle still called her "Queenie," in honor of her deed, she realized now how that one moment of courage failed to hold a candle to the hours and days and years of suffering the people she had helped had endured.

Cooper's cough tugged her thoughts back to him. His jaw worked, and his lower lip trembled a bit.

"You best get yourself tucked back in bed."

He didn't move. When he lifted his face, she sensed that he had made some kind of decision. One that cost him much. She opened her mouth to put the question to him, but his words cut her off. "He's a good man for you, Marylu. You best not push him away."

She stiffened. "What you mean 'push him away?' I didn't push anyone away."

Cooper's gaze went dark and intense, and she thought she caught a sheen of wetness there, but he put a fist to the table and shoved to his feet faster than she'd seen him move in a long time.

"Cooper?"

He disappeared without answering.

fourteen

Chester faced the boy who sat, back up against the wall, beside his bed. He swung his legs over the side and sat up. Zedikiah looked pale in the morning light, and from the stench of him, Chester knew the boy'd already been sick.

"Get cleaned up," Chester admonished as he crossed the room. He splashed water from the basin into the bowl and held out a threadbare towel.

Zedikiah moved really slowly but took the towel and got to work.

"Do your mama proud."

Zedikiah stared at him, towel dripping a stream of water into the basin.

"No drink." He handed the boy the sliver of soap and watched him work it into the towel.

When he finished wiping his face, Chester gestured to him to take off his clothes.

As the morning sun lifted higher in the sky, he scrubbed Zedikiah's clothes out behind the hotel, until the water ran clear. He wrung out the material and strung the shirt and trousers along a fence. All the while a little clock ticked in his head letting him know he had little time before the sun would be high in the sky and the heat would make his hike to Mercersburg miserable.

Chester returned to his room, the coolness there a welcome respite from the humidity swelling with every passing minute.

Zedikiah sat on the bed, the blanket sheathing his slender frame. He lifted his eyes to Chester. "She left me all alone."

He had wondered if the boy would respond to his earlier admonitions.

Sorrow drenched Zedikiah's simple statement. "What am I supposed to do?"

"Not this," Chester said then mimed raising a bottle to his lips. He shook his head and raised a finger toward the ceiling. "See you. She sad." He tried the last word again to make it clearer.

Zedikiah shifted, and his hands came out to cup his head. Sobs rolled out in waves.

Chester went to his knees to hold the boy close. How he wished for a tongue fleet with words to tell the boy his story.

Lord? He sent the silent plea for help and wisdom. How could he make Zedikiah understand?

He gripped the boy's upper arms and held him. When he caught Zedikiah's gaze, he pointed at his heart then at Zedikiah's. "Understand." Again, he mimed lifting a bottle and pressed a hand to his chest.

The boy's eyes went wide with surprise. "You drank, too?"

Chester did his best to convey with hand motions and a few words his entire tale, pleased to see Zedikiah's rapt attention. He ended with the repeated admonition to "Do mama proud."

The slender form lowered his eyes and scuffed his feet against the bare wood floor. "How?" he mumbled.

Chester reached out to place his hand on the boy's shoulder and squeezed. "Be man now. Work hard." As his tongue gave utterance, a swirl of thoughts frenzied his mind. *He* was his own man. Had been since the day he hovered over his father's grave and made the decision to leave home. Through the dark days of slavery, he had longed for his family, sure, and he'd found a measure of comfort in going to church.

People offered him comfort. Lily, who had nursed him back after his first whipping, especially thrilled his heart. She had been a strong woman. Beautiful, but matured beyond her years by the work and conditions. Just when he had thought to love her, she had been sold to someone down in Mississippi.

He'd been devastated and had welcomed the new arrival of another slave and the change in position from field-worker to carpenter for the big house. Samuel's presence had felt like an answer to his prayer for a friend. Someone to offer support and a distraction from the long days. Then the knife had been turned in his gut by Sam's betrayal.

Somewhere in his days running, he had learned to blame God for that. And though hunted, he was free. His freedom had been assured not by some fancy document with broad promises but by hiding himself day and night. Stealing what he needed.

Chester bowed his head, troubled by it all, and the clock in his mind ticked louder. He squinted into the sunshine streaming through the window. As soon as Zedikiah's clothes dried, he would leave. First, he would talk to Mr. Shillito. Perhaps the man would be willing to help Zedikiah find work.

❧

"What you mean you're taking his place?" Marylu sputtered. She eyed Zedikiah and frowned. For all appearances, the boy seemed sober, and the usual reek of alcohol didn't saturate his clothes. And he was smiling.

"Chester made it work with Mr. Shillito that I could take his place while he took care of some things."

"He left?"

"Didn't rightly say where he was going."

Marylu stared at Zedikiah. She pressed her hands together to still the trembling. "Did he—" She cleared her throat. "Did he tell you to tell me anything?"

Zedikiah bent to haul a trunk onto his back. The weight didn't allow him to straighten completely. "Nope," he grunted.

Marylu stepped out of his path but followed him down the steps to the first level and out to the road, where he loaded the heavy trunk into the back of a farm wagon. It amazed her to see the young man bending his back to any work after the many times she had heard reports of storekeepers finding him drunk in front of their shops or in alleys. "You're doing his job?"

He passed her, nodding his head as he went. "Yes, Miss Marylu." Zedikiah turned his face away, but she could see the tendons in his jaw jump. "Chester wanted me to have the chance to prove myself. Told me to be my own man. Someone my mama would be proud of." He sniffed and ran a sleeve across his nose. "Aim to do just that."

"Then you'll be needing some help."

He stared at her, his brows lifted in question. "Help?"

The conviction churned deeper in Marylu's heart. She didn't know where Chester was or if he'd ever return, but she felt sure God was telling her to stop chiding this boy and start lifting a hand to help him. She felt the bite of her conscience that she should have stopped chiding him long ago and, instead, offered to help him work out a plan for his future. He was only a boy. A confused and lonely boy.

Why didn't I see that before?

If he refused her help now and laughed in her face for the tongue-lashings she'd handed out to him, not to mention the time she'd dunked him in that water tank, then she would have to work it through his head how sorry she was for being so blind to his needs. "We'll start by getting you some new clothes and some food to eat."

Zedikiah's nostrils flared, and he glanced away and licked his lips.

Emotion swelled in her throat, and she felt the nudging of the Spirit. "I'm sorry, Zedikiah. Should have been helping you all along instead of being so pleased to make a spectacle of you." She invited him for supper and made a mental note to work up a new pair of trousers for him.

But biting at her mind hardest was not Zedikiah's plight but Chester's departure. Had she pushed him away as Cooper suggested?

When she finally crossed over to Jenny's shop and opened

the back door, she knew immediately that she needed to talk. Jenny would listen and help her see things clearly. She scooted down the short corridor that led to the main room, the voices of customers muffling her desire to burst in and spill all the details, fears, and frustrations.

It took a minute for the voices to register. A man's voice. Marylu tiptoed and peeked around the corner into the main area of the dress shop.

Jenny sat with a bolt of material in her lap and a smile on her lips as she gazed up into the eyes of Aaron Walck.

fifteen

It about killed Marylu to stay out of the main room with Aaron there. She wanted so badly to know why he was setting foot in a dress shop. Alone. A thousand possibilities streamed through her mind. Instead of stewing, she decided to take action.

She slipped into the smaller room that was used for the ladies to change and scanned the board wall for knotholes. She'd studied that wall enough to know the pine boards had them scattered all over. She pushed on each knot to see if any would work loose. The first three she tried didn't budge, but the fourth, far down on the wall, popped out into the room beyond. She held her breath in hopes it wouldn't make a loud sound as it hit the floor.

She bent her left knee first, careful not to lower herself too fast lest the pain be intense, and sunk to the floor. As soon as she caught a glimpse of Jenny and Aaron, she knew that knot could have clattered and clanged up a storm and they wouldn't have noticed. How could two people so right for each other not see it for themselves?

Aaron was handing over some coins, and Jenny was taking them with a grateful, pink-cheeked smile. The man cleared his throat. "I hope you have a good day, Miss McGreary."

"Thank you," Miss Jenny responded in a breathless rush that made Marylu roll her eyes. "You have a good day, too, Mr. Walck."

Vexed at having gone to all the trouble to hear their conversation only to catch the end of it, Marylu got vertical and went out into the main room as fast as her legs could carry her.

Jenny gasped at the sight of her. "Marylu!"

"I saw him here, and you're going to tell me every bit the reason why he came over here."

Jenny's eyes went wide, and she covered her pink cheeks with her hands. "I should have known you were spying on us."

"Not spying." She sputtered to an indignant stop and realized that she had been spying. "Well, not at first anyhow. Got here and heard his voice. When I peeked and saw it was him, I. . ."

Jenny looked over her shoulder at the wall behind her and the knothole in the center of the floor. Her eyes smiled up at Marylu. "I thought I heard something fall. I hope you didn't hurt your knees too much."

Marylu crossed her arms.

Jenny giggled and rolled up the dark material she had spread across her lap. "I couldn't believe it when I saw him walk in. But there he was."

"Your cheeks are pinker than I've seen them since you had the fever two years ago."

She pressed a hand to her face. "Yes, I suppose they are."

"So you going to tell me what he was doing here, or am I going to have to go ask *him*?"

Jenny released a sigh, and her expression sobered a bit. "It was nothing, really."

"*Nothing* didn't seem to be what I was seeing."

With the bolt in her arms, Jenny got to her feet and replaced it in its spot against one wall. "He said he felt badly about the dress and offered to pay me for the material."

"Seemed like he said a whole lot more than that in the time he was here."

"Oh, we talked about the show. He asked me if I was going, and I told him no, that I had work to do."

"Did he say if he was going?"

Jenny brushed a hand across the striped material of Sally's dress. "He was. He wanted to see Eddie perform again. He admires the man's singing."

"Just like you do."

"Yes." There was a wistful clip to Jenny's voice that wasn't hard to translate.

"He say if he was going with Sally?"

"No, and I didn't ask since she already said they were going together."

"After he saw the way she treated you, I thought maybe he'd be smart and change his mind."

Jenny shrugged. "Maybe he feels it wouldn't be the gentlemanly thing to do."

Marylu snorted.

Jenny made a face at her, but when she lifted the striped material, a wistful expression bloomed.

"You know how much you enjoy hearing that young Baer fellow sing."

"It's a minstrel show, so it won't be all about him." Mirth played along Jenny's lips. "And what's this I hear about you being riled up over Chester?"

"Cooper been running his mouth again?"

Jenny tilted her head. "Cooper cares about you. He always has. And you're avoiding my question."

"What question?"

"The one that's killing you."

Marylu licked her lips and pulled in a deep breath. "I'm worried about Chester. He left."

"Then go look for him."

"I don't know where he went."

Jenny laid aside the striped material. "Maybe you had better start from the beginning." She picked up another piece of plain navy cotton and shook it out. Settling in front of the Singer sewing machine, she worked to position it under the needle and smoothed wrinkles with her fingers. "I'm listening."

"I thought Cooper filled your ears."

"Oh, he did, but I want to hear it from you."

But something stirred around in Marylu's mind, and she determined to have her say on the matter before launching into the story of Chester. She moved to the wooden table where Jenny had laid the striped material. "Didn't you say Mr. Walck paid you for the dress Sally left?" She picked up the basted dress and held it up. Since Jenny was slight of form and shorter than Sally, her idea would work.

"Yes. He insisted."

"Then why don't we make it up for you? You go to that minstrel show and show Sally Worth a thing or two." Marylu clutched it to herself. "Since it's just basted together, we can try it on you, then I'll hem it and make final adjustments." She smiled at Jenny. "You'll be so beautiful that Aaron Walck will leave Sally Worth's side and come a-runnin'."

Jenny's laughter split the air. "Probably not, but it is lovely material. You've done wonderful work."

"Who do you think it was who sewed all those little dresses for you growing up?"

"My mother, of course."

Marylu chuckled. "You believe that if you want, but I've got enough pinpricks in these here fingers to prove otherwise."

Jenny hesitated. Her eyes met Marylu's. "You really think I should?"

Marylu crossed her arms and grinned. "Sure as Cooper's going bald."

With a wide grin splitting her face, Marylu followed a determined Jenny to the back room. As soon as the dress swirled down around her friend's slim frame, she knew the dress was perfect. Jenny gave a little gasp of excitement when she saw herself in the mirror, and even did a little preening. Her friend looked anything but plain now. With the pink in her cheeks and her eyes bright with unbridled joy, Marylu swelled with pride.

"Yes, ma'am. That Aaron Walck is going to forget Sally Worth right quick when he lays eyes on you." Marylu left Jenny to change and took the material straight to the chair in front of their Model 15 machine and set to work on the seams.

As her fingers guided the material, her mind went to Aaron Walck and the wistful expression on Jenny's face as she talked of the man. Shy or not, Marylu was sure he'd seen something distasteful in Sally, else why would he feel badly enough to offer to pay for the material? Maybe he didn't know how to handle the situation with her. He seemed the sort who would be unsure of himself in such matters, or maybe he just wasn't sure how Jenny felt, whereas half the town knew Sally's feelings.

"Seems to me two people can come right out and tell each other how they feel without all this mooning," she muttered to herself. When she realized what she'd just said, she stopped pedaling and let the machine go silent. *I'm a fool.*

The sound of Jenny's footsteps shattered her private reprimand. She knew what was coming. Sadness gripped her anew. She tugged the material around to begin sewing a new seam and worked the pedal to get the machine going. Jenny would nail her hide to the wall. She knew it for certain and didn't relish the conversation. Being a realist, Jenny could give sympathy, but the moment she felt someone hadn't made the best of a situation, her patience became short. Marylu closed her eyes and wondered if she had truly put off Chester. If he would ever return. Was he even thinking about her? Oh, to rewind time and get a second chance.

Jenny poked her head around the corner. "Marylu, I almost forgot, Lydia Redgrave's order needs to be delivered."

"Thought she was going to come get it."

Jenny disappeared again, and Marylu heard her rustling around in the back, no doubt locating the two dresses of Lydia's order. When she reappeared, box in her arms, Marylu took them from her and noted the sparkle in her friend's eyes. Part of her wanted to bring up Chester, but the other half held back and eventually won out. Let her friend enjoy the moment. They could talk later.

Jenny took Marylu's place at the sewing machine.

"You going to work on that while I'm gone?" Marylu asked.

"Yes." Her head bobbed, and her foot began to pump the pedal.

When Marylu got out into the sunshine, boxes filling her arms, she thought of Sally's boldness and what the young woman would do if she ever discovered Aaron had visited Jenny. As she crossed Baltimore Street, a train whistle rent the air and pulled past the square of Greencastle. And a plan formed in Marylu's head. If Miss Jenny wouldn't come right out and tell Aaron Walck how she felt, then Marylu would take matters into her own two, quite capable, hands.

&

If Aaron Walck thought it strange to see Marylu at his factory, he didn't let on. If she'd had the choice, she would have gotten Cooper to do this bit of "man-to-man" for her, but his being down nipped that idea in the bud. Besides, some things a woman should handle.

No doubt about it, Aaron Walck was as handsome a white man as Marylu had ever laid eyes on. His dark hair prompted a body to think the man would have dark eyes to match, so when Aaron blinked up at Marylu, his light gray eyes, made even paler in the ribbon of sunshine, were a bit startling. And no Sally hanging on his arm. Which is the other reason Marylu had chosen to come to Aaron's factory instead of meeting him at his house or church or, worst of all, at the Hamlin Wizard Oil Company's minstrel show.

"Good morning, Marylu."

She liked the way the man smiled, as if life were too short for grousing about hard work and long days. Marylu nodded and got straight to the point. "I know you've been hoping for Sally Worth's company at the Town Hall show. She's been singing about it to Miss Jenny for the last week."

Aaron's dark brows drew together when Marylu paused for breath.

"Anyways, I just came here to tell you right out that she is a hard worker and thinks you're a wonderful, kindhearted man. She always had great admiration for what she saw between you and your wife."

Since there was no machinery in this part of the shop,

only a desk, a potbellied stove, and a coal bin, every word she said could be heard. She only hoped that the three men busily working on crafting slender pieces of wood, as another measured out some pieces against a pattern drawn on the floor, would keep what they heard to themselves.

Aaron grunted and glanced at the men, then back at Marylu. "You came here to let me know about Miss Worth or about Miss McGreary?"

"I just wanted you to give Miss Jenny a chance."

This time the color flooded Aaron's face, and he cleared his throat as he got to his feet. He motioned Marylu outside.

Sunshine steamed Marylu's skin pretty quickly, and she aimed herself at a copse of trees where they could carry on a conversation in the shade, away from listening ears.

Aaron leaned against a tall oak and crossed his arms, an amused smile curving his lips. "Are you trying to tell me to court Miss McGreary?"

"No, sir. Knowing grief the way I do, I can't tell you who to court or when to court, but if you're ready to be looking, I am suggesting you at least look Miss Jenny's way."

"And you're discouraging me from. . .*courting*," the word came out hard, "Sally Worth."

"Since you say it that way, yes. There are much nicer women."

Aaron looked away and swallowed. Then a chuckle broke loose, followed by another. Before Marylu knew it, the man was laughing as if a comedy act was being performed before him.

She'd always known Aaron Walck to be soft-spoken, so his laughter at a subject so close to her heart miffed Marylu. She planted her hands on her hips.

He caught her gesture and held up a hand. "I'm sorry, Marylu. It's just so. . ."

Marylu grunted.

Aaron straightened, though a smile still played along his lips. "Sally and I are not courting. Not even close. She asked me to the minstrel show."

It was as if a load of bricks had slid off her shoulders and toppled to her feet. "Why, that's right good news."

"I accepted because. . ." He averted his face, but she saw the mischief die and the sudden rush of grief that cinched his features.

"No need to explain," she offered. "I understand loneliness."

He nodded. "My wife thought a great deal of Miss McGreary's talent and counted her as a good friend."

"I'm guessing Sally wasn't on her list."

He looked embarrassed. "She was quite a bit younger than my wife."

"Flighty and immature, if you ask me. And if you're a godly man, you won't be trifling with her."

Aaron ran a hand over the rough bark of the tree, but the red in his cheeks reminded her of summer-ripened tomatoes.

She reckoned she'd had her say and decided it best for her to leave. "That's all I came for. No need to be letting on that we had this conversation. I love Miss Jenny, and, if I might talk so bold, I've seen the way you look at each other, like butter on biscuits. And there's no sense in wasting time with all the preliminaries when you know a person's heart. Miss Jenny is powerful lonely, and you being lonely, too, well, it only seems natural." She wiped her hands down her skirts and turned. "Think on it."

Without waiting for his response, Marylu climbed back into the wagon and got the horse to back up a bit before slapping the reins against the nag's rump to encourage a nice clip.

sixteen

Chester walked west of Greencastle toward Mercersburg. It would take a long time for him to reach the town where he was born, about ten miles of hard walking by his best guess. He patted the paper safely tucked away in his pocket. Mr. Shillito's friend in Mercersburg went by a name unfamiliar to him. His mama might know the man though.

At some point that morning, he had managed to jam a splinter of wood into his index finger. As he walked, he rubbed his thumb over the area where the sliver had lodged deep in his skin. The pain provided focus as he walked in a void of confusion and anger, hurt and fear. His muscles tightened and pulled, but he kept a steady pace. One foot in front of the other. His heart beating hard both made him feel alive and reminded him that his heart might burst and shatter.

Any guilt over leaving Zedikiah had eased when Mr. Shillito agreed to allow the boy to work for him. Chester had no doubt the man would be good to Zedikiah. By this time, Marylu would know he had left town, and he wondered if she cared.

Her rejection had hurt. Yet what had he expected? Did it matter? The fact was only he knew the truth. Samuel's betrayal had been complete by the detail with which he set Chester up. And the loss of his tongue had prevented Chester from defending himself.

When the question had left Marylu's lips, he had hesitated, in shock. How long had she known? Other questions had crowded his mind, but the slowness of his tongue left him at a disadvantage, and he had found it much easier to simply rise and leave.

He paused at the enormous bridge crossing the Conoco-cheague. Water poured and splashed over and around the rocks in its path. A wide river named by the Indians. To the west, he imagined what the skyline of Mercersburg would look like, and his heart raced with excitement at the thought of embracing his mama again.

Trees, capped with their glorious crown of leaves, rustled in the light, early evening breeze as he continued his walk. Eventually the light of day gave over to night. Wan moonlight washed across fields showing full stalks of corn and wheat. Before long the heat of summer would try to burn away the green of the crops.

His feet burned, but he dared not stop. Drawing closer to his goal stoked his need to get there without further delay. No one would be awake in Mercersburg. Not this time of night. He might be better off sleeping in one of the barns or in the cemetery.

He smiled as his mind went over his childhood spent wandering the fields edged by the Tuscarora ridge, splashing in the ample creeks that mottled the countryside. He wondered if old Mr. Brooks still scared the black children with his stories of ghosts and coming to haunt those who did not treat him well in life. He would be old now, Chester realized with a twinge of sadness, probably in his late sixties. Still working the livery at the large stone hotel in the square of Mercersburg.

Chester's thoughts never ranged far from the scents of the night, the urgency of his pace, and the coldness in the pit of his stomach that had nothing to do with hunger. He paused only when he finally laid eyes on the pale white stone structures of the cemetery that marked the beginning of town. Opposite the cemetery, a stark structure with white cornerstones that contrasted with the brick and looked much like the backbone of a skeleton. The thought made him shudder. An innocent structure seemed suddenly foreboding. It had been a college at one time, but he could see no sign now through the darkness.

He tucked his chin to his chest and kept walking. His legs ached, and his back began a dull protest that started at the base of his spine. He went the opposite direction from town, up Linden Street and back to the cemetery where the blacks buried their own. The one where his father had been buried. It had been that dark day, watching his father's coffin lowered by ropes into the gaping hole, when he'd made up his mind to leave home and go out on his own. He wanted adventure and knew another mouth to feed, without benefit of a man to help farm, meant hardship. He had promised her he'd get work and send money home.

He'd been a fool.

As he neared the cemetery he grew cautious. His father's grave seemed to glow brighter than the others, drawing him closer. Beckoning. He went and knelt at the simple wood cross. His mother would never have the money to afford more, but she had insisted on this. Chester ran his fingers over the rough wood, remembering the grief of carving the shape and lashing the pieces together with rawhide strips. He still remembered the feel of the wood against his fingers as he'd stroked down the length of the cross, tears working their way down his cheeks.

Now his knees felt the cool dampness of the spongy soil as it seeped through his trousers where he knelt. Only now did he understand those things his immature mind couldn't grasp then. Deeper truths that only life can teach. Bitter lessons that his mother had hoped to spare him but his youthful insistence had dragged him into.

He raised his face. In the dark of the night, he saw a slight mound of dirt to the right of his father's grave. His heart bunched in his throat. A new grave. To be expected. A cross marked the head of the mound. No flowers.

His eyes scanned the cemetery. Not a lot of room left in the row. The grave could be one of his sisters or maybe even a brother. A child. He swallowed and pushed a fist against his lips. His gaze fastened, again, on the mound beside his father.

Oh, Sweet Jesus, no.

He inhaled a shuttering breath. He had no way of knowing who had been recently buried. No use fretting. He unclenched his fist and forced himself to relax. He took the first step away from the mound and stopped. When he turned, it was as if he was watching someone else. His heart ached for the poor man who knelt at the pile of smooth, fresh dirt. Whose knees became caked with the mud and whose eyes couldn't help but see that the grass had only just begun to gain a foothold.

So near his father. He couldn't shake the thought. His fist closed around a clump of earth and squeezed.

"Mama."

It came out clear, the strained sound having little to do with his tongue and everything to do with the tightness in his throat. His world shifted, and a strange peace covered him with the certainty that his mama now rested. He would not see her again down here. Ever. And with that came the certainty that he would not see her in heaven.

Murder. Stealing. Running.

His fragile peace shattered into a war of fear and self-retribution. He'd been afraid to come home sooner, and that fear had cost him the opportunity to feel her arms around him one more time.

His shoulders shook beneath the burden of guilt. The boy who had left with so much hope and promise returned with nothing more than a coward's heart and blood on his hands. Shattered beneath his insistence to leave home was the swollen promise of yesterday's dreams. Those dreams were all the things his mama wanted for him. For all her children. To rest. To be happy. To work hard and be kind. To help others and be respectful. To love her Lord.

But how? How could he know how to be all that with all the other terrible deeds?

He didn't know how long he knelt there and allowed himself to grieve, but when he went to rise, he was forced to stand for long minutes and rub the numbness from his legs.

When he could finally stumble along, he picked his way down the path from the cemetery to the section of Mercersburg referred to as Africa. His childhood home would be there. Someone, he hoped, that knew him or his family.

seventeen

Marylu knew before she ever went to bed that lying down would not in itself promise sleep. If not for the fact that she'd just checked on Cooper and found him doing logging duty in a thick forest, she would have sat down next to him and talked herself into a stupor in hopes of getting things straight in her head.

At least Cooper seemed to be making a remarkable recovery, enough so that he insisted on getting back to his little cabin for the night. When she'd come home to get the wagon from Zedikiah, she'd caught Cooper helping the boy, and seeming no worse for the work. It had made her proud to see Cooper taking such a shine to the boy.

She turned over in bed and debated on heading into the kitchen, but her knees ached too much to get up. She sighed and fidgeted. The frame released a sharp crack that set her heart to pounding. When her heart slowed its pace, the face of Aaron Walck pierced her conscience. She'd been so sure of visiting him and telling him, straight out, about Jenny. In hindsight, though, she worried. If Jenny ever found out about her little visit. . . If only Aaron weren't so shy and resigned. If Sally Worth wasn't so forward and pretty.

Marylu sighed and rolled to her side. That's when she heard a board creak overhead. Apparently she wasn't the only one struggling to sleep. Energized at the prospect of talking, she whisked back the blanket and padded out of her room. At the foot of the steps, she stared upward and debated the climb, but her knees throbbed a protest, so she let out a long, low whistle.

Sure enough, she heard Jenny's soft steps shuffle across the floor. The bedroom door creaked open, and Jenny poked out her head. "You can't sleep either?"

"My knees won't let me make that climb," Marylu whispered.

Jenny disappeared for a full minute then reappeared in a dressing gown. When she came level with Marylu, she mouthed the word, "Kitchen?"

Marylu shook her head and they headed back to her room. She shut the door and sat on the edge of the bed.

Jenny took the lone chair and tucked her legs beneath her. "I saw Zedikiah with Cooper. He staying there for the night?"

"Cooper even suggested it. Zedikiah worked hard this afternoon."

"He sure ate more than I've seen any man eat before."

"He's young. No mama to cook for him. No daddy to care. Why, a good wind off the mountains would knock him flat." Marylu paused. "Better to see him eat than to drink so much."

Jenny's gaze met hers then flickered away.

Marylu's senses came alert. It was the same feeling she'd gotten the night Jenny and Cooper acted so strange. A secret brewed between those two, she was sure.

"I've been thinking," Jenny said, her words slow, her face averted. "With Cooper so sick, maybe it's not a bad idea if we take in Zedikiah. He could help out and it would give him some structure."

"A family, you mean."

Jenny's eyes snapped to her face, tension in her expression. Marylu recognized the minute her friend made a decision, for the stress in her features eased. "Tell me about Chester." Jenny asked, "Did you find him?"

For a moment, Marylu hesitated, not sure if she should let the subject go that quickly. If Jenny knew something and didn't want to share, it would be unfair of her to push. But her curiosity had deepened all the more as she had watched the two share guilty glances and flash warnings at each other over the last few weeks. She'd had about enough of it.

"Marylu?" Jenny's smile was tenuous. "I asked about Chester."

She raised her chin and met Jenny's gaze head-on. If her friend didn't want to share, then the decision was made, and she would not push. Yet. "I couldn't find him. I went every place I could think after our talk and...nothing."

"Did he hop a train? Wasn't that the way he got here?"

There it was. Her deepest fear laid bare. If Chester left Greencastle to avoid further questions, it would be the ultimate defeat to her heart. It was too much like Walter's good-bye. A simple, "I love you," then gone the next day.

All thoughts of Cooper and Zedikiah, of the unspoken secret Jenny held so closely, faded beneath the wrench of her frustration. Her anger. She closed her eyes, not realizing she was crying until Jenny moved to sit beside her on the bed.

"Don't cry, Marylu. Please don't cry."

"It's like Walter all over again."

"Shh. I'm sure he's around here somewhere."

But the ring of conviction was not in that statement. Marylu buried her head in her hands and choked on a sob. "What is wrong with me that I can't have no man love me enough to stay?"

⁂

"Mama knew you'd come back when you were ready." Chester's youngest sister sat across from him on the rough wooden bench he remembered so well from his childhood, in the kitchen that had changed little over the years. Ruth, now a grown woman, held out her hands.

He settled his, palms up, into hers.

She turned up the lantern and pulled it closer, then squinted hard at the swollen part on his index finger. "It's deep."

He nodded and continued to study his sister's calm demeanor.

No hysterics or tears when she had discovered him in a corner of the porch before the sun came up. She merely led him inside and set about slicing salt pork and tearing off a hunk of cornbread. "Don't need to know your story. You're home. That's all that matters to me, and all that would have mattered to Mama," had been the first words out of her mouth as she slid the plate in front of him.

In his halting voice, he had explained a bit of his journey and the part about the tongue, leaving out the part about Samuel and the murder, but she'd already heard the rumors.

"Broke Mama's heart, but she insisted until she breathed her last that her boy couldn't do such a thing unless riled up."

Shame washed through him. Why had he thought staying away would keep the news from her ears? In morbid fascination, Chester watched as his sister lowered the needle to his finger and started to poke around.

Her talk filled the uncomfortable space between them. "She died about four months ago. In the cold of winter. Snowed the day we put her in the ground."

Snow. How his mama loved her snow. More than anything he suspected she loved the blessing of a warm home and her family close.

His sister pulled out the splinter and held it up. Their gazes held. Guilt pressed a heavy mist in his eyes that blurred her image. The next thing he knew, her arms wrapped around him, and she cradled his head against her shoulder. Sorrow poured through him and spilled out on Ruth's shoulder. A grown man, crying on the slim shoulders of his little sister, he tried to chide himself. But Ruth's arms encouraged him to grieve harder. He stayed there until the distinct sound of small feet brought him upright.

Ruth rose and skirted about with the efficiency of a woman in command of her kitchen.

Two small bodies appeared. When the smallest laid eyes on him, her eyes went wide. The older, taller boy put a hand to the girl's arm and tensed as if ready to defend.

"Get on over here and eat. Your Uncle Chester has come back after a long time. You can talk his ears off for a change."

Chester wondered if a father would appear, but the way Ruth sat down and the little heads immediately joined her in bowing to give thanks told him this was a normal routine.

"Your uncle is a little slow in his speech, so listen close," Ruth admonished her children as she broke off a corner of cornbread. She popped the morsel into her mouth, caught the gaze of the boy, and nodded at him to indicate he should talk.

The boy's hands stilled, and his eyes sunk to his lap. "My name is Daniel," came the small voice. "I'm eleven."

Chester reached out and rubbed his hand over the boy's head. He turned to the little girl and tried his voice. "You five?" His tongue felt thicker than it did in Marylu's presence.

The two children stared at him.

Embarrassed at the sound of his words, he sent a pleading look to Ruth. Her attention was focused on the little girl. "You understand?"

The girl nodded. Her eyes flicked to him then at her mama, who nodded encouragement.

"I'm seven, and I'm Esther."

Conversation picked up around the table as the children began to share more and more, shedding their shyness and waiting patiently as he tried to work his tongue.

Ruth dismissed them to their chores, and Esther's little groan of protest brought a swift reprimand.

Chester asked the question that begged an answer and watched his sister's expression sag into grief.

"Eddy." She wiped at the lone tear on her cheek. "He got real sick. Never the same after that. He died within a month."

So much sadness and grief. As Chester moved to touch his sister's hand, he felt the burden of her hardship shift to his shoulders and wondered if this was why God had brought him home again.

eighteen

Through the long night, Jenny had offered what comfort she could, but the words stopped penetrating Marylu's discouragement.

She berated herself over and again as she cleaned rooms at Antrim House for asking the question to Chester in the way she had. She'd known the rumors, and she'd known the man. Nothing else mattered.

Or nothing else *should* matter.

But it did matter. To her. And that was what tied her up in knots. Cooper's explanation justified Chester's deeds but didn't excuse it. Or did it?

But what about those gentle eyes? They told another story. Except the shadows she sometimes saw deep in the depths of Chester's gaze, she might never have guessed his past held such violence or that he was capable of anything more than tender touches and teasing mischief.

A streak of brightness came in the form of Zedikiah. At breakfast, his bright, clear eyes had provided the sliver of encouragement Marylu needed. The boy had eaten like a starving man, and she'd been more than happy to see it. At Antrim House, he had seemed intent on his work and content in his skin.

When she finally left the hotel, her thoughts were no more settled than they had been since she had asked Chester the fateful question. She crossed Baltimore Street to Jenny's shop and skirted around to the back door. Jenny greeted her with a preoccupied smile and returned to her sewing machine. Too restless to sit and sew, Marylu decided to tackle cleaning the floors in the back room. There, in a modicum of silence, she gave voice to song after song. Old hymns from church. It helped keep her mind on something other than Chester.

After Marylu finished cleaning half the floor, Jenny appeared in the doorway. "I needed a break from the close work, and it was lonely in there."

Marylu dipped her brush and continued scrubbing, at a loss for words. Tired.

"You're lost in your own thinking and singing to avoid it all, and that spells trouble," came Jenny's observation.

She couldn't look her friend in the eyes. "Not done much else but think."

"He's around here somewhere, Marylu. I just know it. He'll turn up."

"That's what I'm afraid of."

Jenny's eyes widened. "You're afraid he *is* around?"

Marylu didn't know how to explain. She sat back on her heels and wiped her wet hands together. "Don't know what to think. I do know I best be busy, or my head might explode from all this thinking."

"You're worried."

It wasn't the words but the way Jenny said them that stopped Marylu for the second time and forced her to take a hard look at her friend. "It's like I said last night. It's like Walter all over again." She bit down on the words and swallowed hard.

"It's not the worrying that I find so strange. It's your inaction."

This time Marylu was confused. "Done asked after that man all over town. Don't rightly know what else there is to do but pray and wait."

Jenny's skirts swished over the wet floor.

Marylu shooed her back with her hand. "Gonna drag your hem right through—"

But Jenny knelt right down on the floor beside Marylu and grasped her elbows. "Listen to me, Marylu. You've got a chance, don't you see? He's out there. Somewhere. You don't need to be here scrubbing my floors and trying to help me." Jenny's eyes burned into hers. "You need to find Chester.

Whatever fear is stopping you from knocking on every door in this town to find him needs to be put aside."

Marylu didn't know what to say. "I did look. You know that. Couldn't find him anywhere."

"Really? I've never known you to give up so easily, or is it you're afraid to find him?" Jenny squeezed her arms. "Walter hurt you. Real bad. But I've never known you to back down from a challenge, and that's exactly what you're doing now. Walter's going to steal your future, and you're going to let him." Jenny's hands fell away, but her gaze remained firm and steely. "That's not the Marylu I know. That's not the woman who risked her life to set free a wagon full of frightened blacks and helped hundreds get north." Jenny's eyes burned into hers. "Whether he knows it or not, Chester needs you. And you need him."

&

Chester heaved the ax into the stump. He wiped sweat from his brow and breathed deeply of the warm afternoon air. He'd chopped wood for two hours. Ruth now had a long cord of split logs snugged up against the side of the dilapidated stable that housed the cow and horse in the colder months.

Repairs. So many things needed to be done, and he had spent most of his time splitting logs putting it all into a mental list. Repairing the chicken coop would be next. After that, patching the stable. The log house seemed in good shape. For now. He had no doubt the roof leaked in places, evidenced by the water spots on the floor in the room the children shared, but with summer well in place, a few well-placed pots would buy him some time. He could work for weeks and still not be done. And he needed to look up the man Mr. Shillito knew and secure a paying job.

Chester swallowed over the dryness in his throat, longing for a drink. He wondered how Zedikiah fared under Mr. Shillito's guidance. He hoped the boy stayed sober and that someone else would take interest in him. It tugged on him that he should let Cooper know where he had gone. His friend might worry. He owed him some sort of explanation. Chester flexed his fingers. He could write a letter and send it with someone headed toward Greencastle. Explain about Ruth's need, and that his original intention in coming to Greencastle had been to get to Mercersburg and check on the family he hadn't seen in so many years. Cooper would understand.

It was Marylu who wouldn't understand.

Marylu.

Chester stretched upward to relieve the dull ache in his back and pulled a suspender back into place. He closed his eyes. *Marylu.*

"You've got a lot done," Ruth called from the garden, where she worked the plow deep into the ground. Her gaze raked over him then the pile stacked against the shed. "Not too bad for an old man."

Chester stretched, his legs stiff from last night's long walk, too little sleep, and too much wood chopping.

Ruth left the plow and headed toward the house. She lifted her head. "Daniel! Esther!" Her voice rang out across the yard that separated her from the structure where the children worked inside.

Esther's head poked out from an upstairs window. "Daniel's beating the rug, Mama."

"When he's done, I'm wanting him to plow. Your uncle is needing a drink. Get one for him, little gal."

"Yes, Mama."

Ruth glanced back at him and pointed to the front step, shaded by a huge oak tree.

Sweat trickled down his back, and he gratefully accepted the prospect of the cool spot. As he settled himself on the step, Esther appeared with a tin of cold water. He gulped it down, uncaring of the droplets running down from the corners of his mouth. When he offered the empty tin to Esther, she smiled, took it, and scurried off.

Ruth sat beside him, her face in profile. He recognized

that profile, a twin to his mother's, and the reminder was a physical ache. "You going to be moving on or staying?"

He gave the question some thought and realized with a heavy heart that the answer had less to do with him than it did with her. If he left, she would be alone again. If he stayed, she would have someone to help. To trust and depend upon.

Writing a letter would be slow work. He could get to Greencastle and back in short order and still have plenty of daylight to finish up work and get started on his search for a job. He could make sure Cooper's cough was better and that Zedikiah was staying out of trouble. Say good-bye to Marylu. "I need go Greencastle. Horse?"

Ruth's gaze missed nothing. "Something there you need to take care of?"

He nodded.

Her dark eyes flashed. "You been wandering a long time. Mama feared you were dead."

Chester leaned forward and cradled his head in his hands. He had hidden for good reason, she must understand that. Coming home would have brought trouble to his family, and he couldn't bear seeing his mother's face and confessing his deed.

No, he had walked steadily west and north in those days, always on the alert, always afraid. It choked him even now, that icy feeling that at any moment the dogs would be on him and sink their teeth into his flesh, followed by their master. Forcing his mind from the past, he lifted his head to the sky.

"After hearing of the master being slain, she reckoned you were too ashamed to come back."

Chester didn't look at her. The truth laid bare his soul. How his mama had known him.

Ruth's gaze turned soulful. "She wanted me to give you something." She pushed to her feet, the step letting out a moan at the release of the weight upon it.

She left him alone. And he had all the time he needed to

consider what it might be that Mama wanted him to have. Her favored possessions had been few and precious and probably things better left for Ruth to give to her children. Her Bible, for one, would be the thing his mama would hold dearest. The legacy for her children and a silent admonition to look to Him for direction on the paths they chose.

He heard Ruth's steps drawing nearer and looked up as she came into view. In her hands she held the Bible. A lump solidified in his throat.

She held it out to him.

He shook his head and pushed its cool leather cover away. "Give to babies."

She grasped his wrist, her rough skin scratching against his, and laid the volume on his palm. "She wanted Daniel to have it, but there is something inside that is for you."

Chester's heart hammered, and he saw, for the first time, the way the cover of the Bible humped over a bulky object pressed within. Curiosity ran parallel to the great sadness that threatened to overwhelm him.

"Open it," Ruth's voice, both soft and hard in tone, admonished him.

He gulped and blinked to relieve the blurriness in his vision. He pushed his finger into the cavity where the bulky object lay and flipped the pages open. His breath stopped. A storm of emotion billowed and blew through him as his trembling hand lifted out the snowy white kerchief, edges laced with delicate embroidery. In slow motion he lifted it to his face as images flashed through his mind.

His mother's face the day he left.

The handkerchief clutched in her hand.

His first step toward the road.

That moment when he'd paused to look over his shoulder.

He had gulped and fought his fourteen-year-old doubts. He had never seen his mother cry. She had stood, stalwart and seemingly immovable, eyes resigned to his decision to leave. He knew then that she would not beg him to stay.

Would never resort to hysterics or open displays of grief. She would remain detached, yet attached to his heart always. Still, the little boy in him wanted to see evidence of sorrow.

He had forced his eyes forward and kept them on the road a few more steps, before the urge to look back and freeze her image into his brain for the long days ahead gripped him and he turned. She still stood there, her hands lowered now, her features blurred by the distance between them.

Another step. Then another. At the end of the dirt road, right before it turned to wind out of sight, he had given one last glance over his shoulder, and that's when he had seen her, handkerchief raised to her face. He'd known then how much she loved him and would miss him. He had stopped on the path, torn between running back to the only safe haven he had known and making his own way. Only the need to lessen her burden kept him moving, to make more of himself so he could send money back and help her.

Chester's breath rattled as the memories crashed in, and he stroked the soft material against his cheek. The handkerchief, a symbol of her love for him, of her grief and sorrow, and a hundred other emotions that she never gave voice to but were there. . .and all for him.

Chester clenched his fist around the delicate fabric and struggled against another wave of tears as they burned for release. He shoved himself vertical and took quick steps away from the porch, unconsciously heading down the same path he'd taken that day.

And only then did he release his tears, adding to the cloth the salt of his grief that mirrored the salt of grief his mother had released so many years ago.

nineteen

Ruth pushed a cup of hot coffee across to Chester. Rain pattered against the glass of the kitchen window. He wrapped his hands around the tin. His stomach full of warm food, his heart full of the residue of laughter he had shared with his niece and nephew before Ruth had shooed them off to bed, bowls in their hands.

She had paused at the base of the stairs and called up a reminder. "Daniel, you make sure Esther sets her bowl right under the leak."

"Yes, Mama."

Chester felt a grin. Some things never changed. Ruth sounded just like their mama, who had liberally tossed last-minute warnings or reprimands up the staircase after they'd gone up to bed.

He could tell the minute Ruth finally relaxed. Her shoulders slumped forward, and her eyelids became heavier than before. The sight of her exhaustion stirred something within him.

"I take"—he stumbled badly over the hard T—"care of you."

Ruth's gaze snapped to him. "No."

He flinched at the hardness of that single syllable.

"You've your own life to live. I'll not be taking you from that."

He struggled for an answer.

She never gave him the chance. "Daniel will resent you being here. He's used to doing hard work." She held her hand out to him across the table, her expression placating. "You've got to understand, Chester. I'm a woman quite capable of making my own way. Daniel and Esther need to know hard work. If you're around it could get too easy."

He reluctantly took her hand, her way of offering appreciation for his offer. And in some strange way, he understood her fear. She didn't want to become dependent on others. Still, he had to try. He lifted his free hand, pointed to her then to himself. "Family help each other."

"You've got a life ahead of you. Live it."

"Just me, Ruth."

Her eyes shifted over his face, and he felt that same deep-thinking demeanor he had often witnessed in their mother. As if she could read his mind and thoughts. His heart.

"You haven't ever loved?"

He opened his mouth to utter a protest, but his throat closed on the word.

"You spent over a month in Greencastle before getting over here. Why? Why wouldn't a man who's been gone so long get right over to the place where his family was when he got so close?"

"Got some work." But the words fell flat when her gaze continued to burn into his. Demanding the truth.

"That's good. Work's good for a body." She released his gaze and stood to open the door. A breeze shifted through the house. It swirled around him and cooled his skin. He lifted the cup to his lips and frowned. The coffee had cooled to lukewarm.

"Go back to Greencastle and work. You can come visit us sometimes."

"I get job here."

Her gaze lifted to some point over his shoulder. "You could. But you don't need to. I do some work for one of the women in town, and she pays good. Other than splitting wood, I can take care of things. Daniel and Esther and myself. . ."

The way she said it got his attention. Daniel. Esther. Ruth. A complete family, yet he sensed she left something unsaid. Another name that needed to be added to the list. He followed her out onto the porch. A lone man came up the dirt road. He lifted his hand as way of greeting, and Ruth returned the gesture. Chester faced Ruth and lifted his eyebrows and smiled.

She jutted out her chin. "He's a good friend."

He snorted.

She flapped her hand at him. "You get on back to Greencastle."

"I'll come visit."

Ruth's smile went wide. "We'll welcome you."

twenty

Marylu set out toward Mercersburg when all else failed. No one had seen hide nor hair of Chester. Several, including Cooper, had told her heading out to Mercersburg would be the place to find him, with him having kin there and all. So, she guided the old horse west on Baltimore Street, at war with herself over not just what she'd say but what to expect should she find him.

Jenny's admonition stuck in her head. Going after Chester was one thing. Admitting to herself that she was drawn to the man meant letting go of hurts and fears that she'd harbored since Walter's good-bye broke her heart. Too, her rejection might mean that he had moved on in his heart.

Out on the road and past the cemetery and then the raging Conococheague, she trotted the horse, forcing her mind away from the problems and doing some praying. Wouldn't do to not let the Lord know her worries and gain the benefit of the peace He wanted her to have. Only when she felt the peace in her soul did she breathe the air into her lungs and realize the good Lord had full control. If she found Chester, she would rejoice. If she didn't, it wouldn't be for lack of trying.

A mile more up the road, with the sun sinking over the Tuscarora ridge in the distance, Marylu saw the outline of a man on the horizon. Walking. Dark skinned. And she knew in her heart who it must be. She pulled back on the reins and slowed the horse. Uncertainty rose, and even though miles separated them, she panicked anew at the idea of seeing him again.

I'm scared, Lord.

❧

Chester left Mercersburg the same way he got there. On foot.

Ruth told him many times to take the horse, but he knew Daniel needed the animal to get back and forth to town, and Ruth needed the animal to help plow the rougher spots.

But he didn't leave without saying good-bye to his mama. Evening shadows cast scary outlines on the gravesites as Chester stood above his mama's grave and repented of his youthful foolishness and his cowardly ways. Still, everything felt twisted up inside him. The load of guilt and fear too much for his shoulders. He longed to be at peace again. If going to church meant peace, he would go. The small church he had gone to in the South, sensing his mama's God so close to him, had failed him somehow. But his mama's voice, her expression unyielding, would tell her children that God never failed.

He closed his eyes, tired in every sinew and tendon. *Lord, I don't know how to do this. Don't even know what I'm supposed to do or if You hear, but I need to know the answer to this here question of mine.*

He moved on in his silent conversation to his mama. He clutched the slightly yellowed kerchief, and when he finished saying a final good-bye, he tucked the square into the little sack his sister had prepared for him and turned his face toward Greencastle.

For better or for worse, he had to go back and explain to Marylu all that had happened with Samuel. He loved her and wanted to believe she would understand his heart and his fight for freedom.

And Zedikiah needed someone. It dawned on him that the burden in his heart had much to do with his belief that God should send someone else to care for the boy. He needed to care for Zedikiah. To guide and help him, and others like him. To be kind, as his mother had taught, gentle, as she had admonished.

Miles down the road, day giving out to darkness, he saw a wagon on the rise coming from Greencastle. He didn't think much on it. One wagon looked much like another. His feet got to hurting, though, and he stopped to rest, grateful the sun was sinking behind him and hoping for a wagon to come by that was headed either to Greencastle or farther on to Waynesboro. Might be he could hop a ride. He raised his face to the wagon heading his direction and wondered if they might be going into Mercersburg with the intent to head back toward Greencastle in the morning. He could sleep in the fields and wait if they'd agree to take him along. Didn't seem much like the driver was in a hurry to get anywhere, though.

Chester rubbed his knees to ease the ache. It felt good to lean over and stretch his back. The wood cutting only added to his overall misery now. He grinned at his aches and pains. In his days down south, he'd worked long hours in the smoking hot sun and never thought a thing about it. He'd grown soft. His smile sagged into a frown. Soft and aimless.

He sucked in the mint-cool evening air and raised his face to the beautiful rainbow colors streaking the sky. When he craned his neck and checked behind him toward the Tuscarora ridge, the intensity of pink and orange danced like a fire on the mountain range, as familiar to him as Mama's corn bread.

Southern sunsets could be as beautiful, but something about this one tonight seemed heavy with promise. He chuckled at the fanciful thought. No different than any other night. Same sun. Same Lord in heaven painting them. Sometimes He let the colors shine through, and other times He let the clouds hide them.

The jangle of wagon wheels crawled toward him as the vehicle got nearer. He turned his head and raised his hand to stop the driver and ask his question, but his gesture froze solid when he recognized the woman behind the reins.

His hand fell to his side, his gaze fixed on Marylu. She didn't look none too happy to see him. Or was that worry tightening her expression?

"You need a ride?"

Her question hung in the air between them. He hesitated. His eyes scanned over her face and searched for any sign of disgust or pity, softness or warmth. He could discern nothing and took a step closer to the wagon. "Saw sister." He gestured over his shoulder to the west. "My mama died."

"I'm sorry. Sorry for her as much as you. I can't imagine losing a son and not setting eyes on him before breathing my last. It must have been terrible for her. And for you."

Her words hammered at him, but the last three softened the blow, and he saw a flicker in her expression that promised warmth.

"Seems we've a lot of talking to do." She twirled the reins through her fingers, then pulled them loose and speared him with a look. "You going to get in this here wagon and get on back with me, or you walking?"

His smile came slowly, building as her lips twitched then began their own upward curve. "Feet hurt." He chuckled.

"Then get up here, and let's go home."

Home.

Sounded good to him.

twenty-one

Chester moved as if to vault himself into the wagon's bed, but Marylu would have none of it and stopped him. "You sit up here with me where we can hear each other. No use hollering back and forth."

What she wasn't prepared for was having him so close. The wagon seat seemed to shrink mightily as soon as Chester took his seat. When he grinned down at her, she lifted the reins and pulled on the right one to bring the horse around, as much to get them headed in the right direction as to cover the rush of warmth his smile pulled from her.

She flicked the reins in unison, and the horse plodded along. "You're headed back to Greencastle?" she blurted, immediately regretting the words. It sounded desperate.

From the corner of her eye, she watched for his reaction, but he didn't move other than the swaying that came with the rhythm of the wagon. "For Cooper. For boy's sake. Mine."

She blinked, unsure what to make of the words. "I'm not sure what you mean."

"No more running." He swallowed and coughed lightly, and she reasoned his throat must be dry after walking so far. When his gaze met hers again, his eyes were soft. "I been a fool. Samuel my friend. He told master I stole."

He paused and looked away. His chin trembled, and the muscles in his cheeks rippled. "I stole nothing."

It came out choked and strained, and Marylu could feel the depth of his emotion. More than that, she understood it. His friend had betrayed him just as Walter had betrayed her heart. She should not be surprised to see the tenderness of Chester's heart regarding his friend's betrayal.

Marylu released pent-up breath, relieved that her instincts

to trust him had not failed her.

"How'd your tongue come to be. . . ?" The words seemed so harsh, but he picked up on her meaning.

"He make it look like I'd stolen. Like I lied. Try cut out tongue. Samuel held me."

"You escaped." Marylu filled in the blank based on Cooper's version of the story.

Chester nodded. "Pain. I went crazy. So hard. Hurt. When knife make cut, I—"

Marylu studied Chester's profile silhouetted against the fading brilliance of evening sky. The cocoa of his skin and the curve of his nose. The shadows under his eyes, cast there by the waning light of day. She pulled back on the reins and made short work of twisting them around the hand brake.

He glanced at her, surprised. She touched his hand. His gaze locked with hers, and she saw the pain there, brought back by reliving his past.

"You listen here," she began. "It wasn't your fault. If you knocked that man back and he was hurting you, it wasn't your fault. Just 'cuz I've lived up here with Miss Jenny's family doesn't mean I've not heard the stories of cruelty. What that man did wasn't right, and Mr. Lincoln told everyone that. Cooper told me some of your story, but I wanted to hear it from you." She paused to gather her words and thoughts. "You're a hero, Chester. More than me because you and all them slaves who suffered and endured were *there*."

"You helped."

She shook her head and placed her free hand against his cheek. His warm skin eased the chill in her fingers, and she closed her eyes for an instant to absorb the touch. When she opened her eyes, she gave him a gentle smile. "I helped. But I've never known suffering like what I saw and heard about from those we helped. Like what you been through."

Tears welled in his eyes, and he swallowed.

Her lips trembled. "Don't you see? It's one thing to see it and hear about it. It's another to live through it and to survive. *You're* a hero, Chester."

A tear spilled down his face, then another. Slowly he lifted his hand and covered hers where it rested against his face. With infinite tenderness, he pulled her hand to his lips and pressed a gentle kiss against her palm.

❧

Chester lowered Marylu's hand and turned her fingers in toward her palm, cupping the kiss he had just pressed there. His heart rejoiced at this woman. At her bravery and her strength and the beautiful words that made his heart soar and dispersed the dark clouds in his soul.

He'd expressed once before his love for her, and those very words rose to his lips now and demanded release, but he held back. What she offered him was enough.

Marylu ducked her head and messed with the reins, and Chester grinned at her embarrassment. Confidence rose like the sun in his heart. To win this woman, he would need to be a man worthy of her.

As the wagon picked up speed, Chester pursed his lips and wondered about Zedikiah. The boy needed the job at Antrim House much worse than he did. Zedikiah needed to feel a sense of self-worth that came with a job well done. Chester stared down at his hands, at the blister on his middle finger, and he realized that, more than anything, he wanted to work with wood again.

"Furniture maker in town?"

Marylu cast a sideways glance at him. "Furniture?"

He nodded.

"A couple. You looking to leave Zedikiah doing your job at the hotel?"

He realized it meant he wouldn't see Marylu in the mornings.

"Sure do have a way with furniture," Marylu said. "The way you got those repairs done at the hotel. Mr. Shillito was impressed, too. He won't be happy to lose you. Cooper will be glad to see you. And Miss Jenny."

Chester looked hard at her profile.

"Zedikiah would be missing you, too."

When she turned her head, he sent her a knowing smile, and the way she jerked her head forward again, intent on the horse's head and then the scenery that surrounded them, only confirmed that Marylu spoke for everyone but herself. It amused him that she found it so difficult to express her own wants.

He chuckled and stretched his arms up in the air. Then, as casually as possible, he settled his left arm on the back of the wagon. Her back brushed up against him with the swaying of the wagon. If she noticed, she didn't let on a mite.

twenty-two

Chester insisted on walking to the hotel from Jenny's house since it was dark when they got back to Greencastle, and Marylu finally agreed. From her place at the window, she watched him rub down the horse and give it grain, his body nothing more than flashes of white from his shirt and the horse's white stockings and blaze face glowing in the night. She pressed her forehead against the cool glass, surprised and pleased at the swiftness of the change in him. The Lord's doing, she knew. Change always came about easiest when the soil of a heart is tilled and loosened for planting.

She pressed her hands to her cheek at the memory of his kiss on her palm and the way he'd planted his arm on the wagon bench behind her. She could not deny the protective feeling she received by his gesture. She had savored every moment of the ride home, quiet talk of nothing more than sunsets and mountains, crops and farmers.

When he came close to the window where she stood and raised his hand, she sighed and blew out the lantern, then crept through the house to her room. It didn't take long before she heard a light knock. She smiled. Miss Jenny would have heard her and want to know everything. She answered as the second knock echoed around the room.

Jenny raised her lantern. "A smile is what I'd hoped to see on your face."

Marylu stepped back, and Jenny squeezed by her and set her lantern on the table before sliding into the chair. Marylu turned to her friend, hands on hips. "Can't a body get some sleep before doing the talking?"

Jenny laughed. "You wouldn't sleep a wink, and you know it."

Marylu settled herself on the foot of her bed. "It's true enough."

"So you found him?"

"On the road from Mercersburg. He was walking."

Jenny tilted her head. "And?"

Marylu savored the story, as much to privately relive the surge of hope as to tease her friend. "We talked, and he told me about the murder he was rumored to have committed."

Jenny listened to the entire story without interrupting. When Marylu mentioned the kiss, her friend's eyes rounded in excitement.

Marylu hid a yawn, but Jenny caught the action and matched it with a yawn of her own. They shared a giggle.

Jenny got to her feet and reclaimed the lantern. "I'm so happy for you."

Marylu's mind went back to her conversation with Aaron Walck, and something else, too. "Tomorrow night is the show." She needed to get Jenny's new dress finished up, which meant she would need to work extra hard at the hotel to gain enough time to get the sewing done.

Jenny nodded. "It will be fun."

There lacked the ring of conviction in her voice, and Marylu knew her friend both dreaded the night and looked forward to it. For herself, she had hoped that Aaron Walck would break off with Sally Worth and run to the dress shop to ask Miss Jenny, but Marylu realized he would probably be too much of a gentleman for such a thing.

She allowed her friend to leave with a whispered, "Sweet dreams," before she remembered Zedikiah.

"Jenny," her whisper shot through the dark. "Is Zedikiah with Cooper?"

The lantern in Jenny's hand cast dancing shadows across her face. She raised it. "No. He left right after you took the wagon to go after Chester."

Marylu thought on that as she settled down for the

evening. The news took the edge of joy from her day as she imagined the boy back out on a drinking binge.

≥∂

Chester's feet protested the walk down Carlisle toward the center square of Greencastle, where he turned left. Antrim House seemed a long way up Baltimore Street to his tired body. The ride from Mercersburg had been worth it, though, not only to spare his body the walk but also for the promise his conversation with Marylu held. She thought him brave and courageous. It brought peace to his troubled mind.

And when he had kissed her palm. . .

She'd been pleased. He was sure of it.

When he finally pushed open the door to his old room, he was relieved to find it empty of Zedikiah. Surely the boy wouldn't deny him a couple of nights on the floor, since he'd done the same thing for him. Chester removed his shirt and stretched out on the floor, leaving the bed for its rightful owner. He released a deep, satisfied sigh.

In the dark he smiled. Then frowned as a scratching sound caught his ear. He stilled. Silence ensued. He curled on his side and closed his eyes again.

Another scrape, louder than the last, jerked him upright. Dread churned deep in his stomach. Zedikiah's face filled his mind and with it a sense of guilt. He should have known as soon as he found the room empty that the boy would be out doing something he shouldn't. Being a hotel, though, it could be nothing more than a restless guest. Chester strained his ear in an effort to pinpoint the direction from which the sound originated.

Out in the hallway, he slipped the door to the outside open a crack. The sound of ragged breathing came to him. He could make out the outline of someone. "Zedikiah?"

The image jerked in answer to the whispered question.

Chester swung the door wider. "Who's there?"

"Mr. Chester, that you?"

Chester's heart raced. "Scare me."

"I thought you were going to be gone longer," Zedikiah whispered.

Chester inhaled the air around the young man, gratified that it didn't reek of alcohol. He reached out to grab the boy's arm and ended up with a fistful of his shirt. Didn't matter though. With a sharp jerk, he hauled Zedikiah into the hallway, then his room, and shut the door. "Where been?"

Zedikiah slumped into the chair and leaned forward. Chester left the boy to his silence to strike a match and light the lantern. When he faced him again, Zedikiah held his head in his hands and was rocking silently back and forth.

The sight caught at Chester, and he pressed his hand onto the boy's shoulder. "Zed?"

He stopped his rocking and turned puffy eyes on Chester. "I was over at the cemetery."

Chester raised his eyebrows in silent question.

"Wanted to get a drink. Needed one real bad. So I went to the only place I knew I'd be safe. Knew Mama would be there, somehow, telling me to be strong."

A shiver went through Zedikiah, and Chester tightened his hold on the boy's shoulder. Instinctively, he knew the tremor was not from cold but from his determination not to drink.

"You tired?"

"Came back here so I'd be ready to work as soon as I got up."

Chester nodded at the news and motioned to the floor.

Zedikiah shook his head. "You sleep on the bed. Wouldn't be right having you sleep on the floor. Mama would haunt me for sure."

Chester tried to protest, but Zedikiah dived down on the floor and shot him a grin.

Chester shrugged and threw him the blanket, wishing he had a pillow to offer. He'd get one tomorrow. "You sleep. Work hard."

Zedikiah blinked up at him, his puffy eyes screaming that

part of the story that his lips did not form.

Chester felt the depth of the boy's struggle for sobriety as much as he did his grief for a mama that loved him.

❧

Sunlight swept across his closed lids and stirred him to wakefulness. Chester cast an eye over the floor, relieved to see Zedikiah still asleep. His grief must have drained him, just as it had drained Chester the previous day.

After pulling on his shirt, Chester toed Zedikiah's side until the young man stirred and opened his eyes. "Clean up," he admonished the boy.

Zedikiah blinked and sat up. He smoothed a hand down his shirt then over his hair.

"Mr. Shillito want good work," he suggested to the boy.

"You back now. Are you going to take over your job?"

Chester shook his head. "I find other job. Work make strong. You man now."

twenty-three

Marylu didn't see Chester at all that morning. But the Zedikiah she saw swelled her heart. Though still a bit scruffy and definitely scrawny looking, he wore a keen expression that Marylu had not witnessed in the boy since before his mother's death. "You didn't come home last night," she grunted to him as he worked to patch a hole in the ceiling. "I got worried."

"You thought I was out drinking."

Taken back by his bluntness, she nodded. "I hoped not."

His chuckle came out dry and mirthless. "Guess I have a long way to go."

She didn't answer, the words sucked away by the change in his attitude. "Chester here?"

"Yup." He braced himself on the ladder and pounded a few nails into a board. "And nope."

"You aim to drive me crazy, don't you?"

Zedikiah's smile was wide. "No, just trying to get this done fast. Mr. Shillito's got a mess of chairs that need repairs. Chester stayed long enough to show me what to do to repair this hole and make it good with Mr. Shillito. He said he'd let me stay so long as Chester agreed to help me know how to make the repairs."

"Well, you come on over for supper tonight. You're going to need your strength to fight the demons at your heels."

Zedikiah frowned down at Marylu. "You gonna help me?"

The fact that he questioned for one minute her willingness to help smote her. With renewed conviction she vowed to pay closer attention to the boy's problems. Drawn to the need in his eyes, she nodded. "I am. Cooper and Miss Jenny, too. We'll all help you. Your mama would want it."

"I know. Chester says the same thing."

It pleased Marylu that Chester wanted to help Zedikiah as much as she did. She missed the idea that she worked in the same building as Chester, but Zedikiah's diligence at the job showed such great promise, not to mention a natural talent with wood.

At the dress shop that afternoon, she worked the pedal of the Singer until Miss Jenny's dress was complete. She took out scissors and began to clip stray threads from the seams.

"Got your dress done for tonight," she hollered toward the back room into which Jenny had disappeared minutes ago.

Between taking orders and trying to keep up with cutting out patterns and sewing, Jenny'd barely had time to sit down. Marylu grinned. Probably so excited about the show that evening that Jenny couldn't sit still if she tried.

Jenny appeared, cheeks rosy with color.

Marylu held up the finished product. "Let's get it on you. Tell me, too, what it is that has you so tickled."

Jenny took the dress and held it up to herself. She stared at it in the mirror for a full minute. Her eyes finally locked on Marylu's. "I saw Aaron today. At Ziegler's."

"Eyeing those new shoes?"

"I was."

"Did you get them?"

"He didn't have my size."

Marylu shook her head. "I told you you should have gotten them last week in time for tonight."

Jenny turned from the mirror and shrugged. "It's too late now." She set the gown aside and picked up an old rag. Maybe she had read her friend wrong after all. That she set aside the gown with such ease and the fact that her expression became pinched did not bode well.

"I can do that," Marylu offered. "You just keep talking about your visit with Aaron Walck."

Jenny swept the cloth down the length of the display case with its pretty assortment of buttons and trims tucked inside.

"There's nothing to tell."

Marylu hesitated. Jenny's sharp tone held rebuke. She raised her eyes to look at her friend and wondered what was causing such turmoil that Jenny would be so sharp.

Her friend paused the rubbing motion and crumbled the rag in her fist. "I'm sorry, Marylu. That wasn't called for. I know you're trying to help me. I just want to go and have fun and not worry about Sally and Aaron."

What it meant to Marylu was that Jenny's run-in with Aaron had not resulted in his asking her to attend the show with him. She had so hoped he would. The day he bought the material would have been fine timing for him to admit Sally was not the one for him, or even today at the hardware store. She huffed. *Lord, in Your time. Not mine.* Though she sure wished the Lord would hurry up anyway.

"You're just feeling a might nervous, that's all. You don't have to tell me nothing."

Jenny's gaze shifted, and her hand began an unconscious circular motion along the display case. "He was kind to me. Even asked if I'd changed my mind about attending the show."

"And you said yes."

"I told him about the dress and thanked him again."

"And you stood there and stared at each other like the two addle-brained lovers you are."

"Marylu!"

"Well, it's true. Just he can't see it quite clear yet. He will, though, you can be sure of that."

"No." Jenny bowed her head, the rag hung from her fingertips. "I don't think he cares. He's probably trying to be kind."

"Kind don't buy a woman a dress."

"He didn't buy it."

"Might as well have," Marylu argued. "He paid for the material."

"Because he is kindhearted. Nothing more."

Marylu hoped with all her soul that it wasn't because he was kind. No, it couldn't be. Not with the way she had seen him look at Jenny that day in the shop. What he needed was another visit from her. A reminder.

Jenny slumped into the chair next to Marylu and covered her eyes. "Do you think there's any hope for me?"

Her friend's voice seemed so small and uncertain. Marylu stabbed her needle into the material and went to Jenny. She put her arms around the woman. "If he can't see the woman that Sally is and the difference between you and her, then you need to be looking elsewhere anyway. I'll not have your heart hurt by a man who can't tell the difference between a woman and a shrew."

"Marylu!"

"Well, it's true. She doesn't hold a candle to you."

Jenny's arms tightened around Marylu. "Thank you, my friend."

twenty-four

Chester raised his hand to knock on the door of Jenny McGreary's house.

Zedikiah answered with a huge grin on his face.

Heartened to see the young man's obvious good cheer, Chester returned his smile and sat down at the table across from Cooper. The spark was back in the older man's eyes. Only on rare occasion did he cough.

Zedikiah slipped in beside Chester and pulled the Bible close.

"Read?" Chester asked.

Zedikiah raised his eyes from the pages of the Bible. "My mama taught me. Miss Marylu taught her."

Cooper leaned forward. "His mama was quite a woman. Reminded me some of our Marylu."

Chester's eyes rolled to the older man. Something about the way Cooper said that, about Zedikiah's mother, set his mind to roiling. How was it that Marylu had never picked up on Cooper's love for her?

Even the way Zedikiah tilted his head at the old man said something. "You knew Mama?"

" 'Course," Cooper snapped. "Most everyone know everyone here in town."

Zedikiah lowered his gaze to the pages.

Chester felt for the boy. Cooper's irritability seemed unwarranted and uncharacteristic. Or maybe it was a side of the old man he was just discovering. "What reading?" He asked Zedikiah to change the subject.

"About King David and Absalom. He got into trouble because he betrayed his father."

Words froze in Chester's mind. *Betrayal*, a word he

understood so well. "Happened?"

"Haven't finished reading it yet." Zedikiah raised his eyes. Chester caught the quick, cautious glance he shot at Cooper. Like a man eyeing a growling, snapping dog.

"Had friend. He betray me."

Zedikiah didn't seem shocked by the news, and Chester figured the boy had heard bits and pieces of his story over the last few weeks. "If you were my daddy, would you tell me?"

Chester saw the earnestness in the boy's expression and understood where the question, in regard to betrayal, had come from. He nodded and squeezed the boy's shoulder. "Be proud to have son like you." He stumbled over the phrase but felt it important that Zedikiah understand his sincerity.

Zedikiah's face crumbled, and he stared down at the Bible again. Chester happened to glance over at Cooper, shocked when he saw the old man fighting tears.

"Cooper proud, too," he added, tapping Zedikiah's hand and indicating Cooper.

But instead of Cooper agreeing, he got up and shuffled out of the room.

Chester shrugged.

Zedikiah seemed nonplussed. "Maybe he's sick again."

Chester didn't think so. Something ate at the man. An idea swirled in his head. He, too, got to his feet. "Where Marylu?"

Zedikiah pointed at the cookstove, where pots bubbled merrily. "She left out the back door to get something from the garden. Probably cabbage." Zedikiah made a face.

Chester chuckled and pushed to his feet. "I'll go. Help her." He stepped out back and into the cool night air. He knew that the garden lay back a ways, to his right. He'd noticed the first sprigs of greenery a couple of weeks ago and seen Cooper working the ground. Now, in the light of the waning moon, he could just make out the form of someone headed his way from that direction.

"When did you get here?" Marylu's voice washed over him as she stepped into the circle of weak light falling through the window. "It's a right good thing I have plenty cooking up in those pots." She stared down into her apron, where a bountiful supply of greens were piled.

"Collards?" Chester questioned.

She nodded at him. "Got some spinach in here, too. Now if you'll just hold that door for me."

He hopped up the steps and did as she bid him to. She lifted her apron onto the table and dumped her bounty out in front of Zedikiah. "Where'd Cooper go?"

"Room," Chester answered before Zedikiah.

Marylu laid eyes on Zedikiah. "You get back to his room and tell him to help you pick through this pile. Separate the spinach from the collards. Wash them up for me, too." She spun on her heel and headed Chester's way.

He threw open the door all over again. "Help?" he asked, as she passed him.

"I could always use an extra pair of hands."

He followed her down the path and out onto the moist, newly plowed soil and across to the patch that held rows of greens.

Chester watched as she leaned down, her fingers tearing at the leaves. "Cooper's a fine hand at planting winter greens, but it takes a mountain to move his body when it comes to harvesting. Guess he feels he's done his work by that time."

He wanted to say something about Cooper's strange reaction but got distracted at the sight of Marylu. The dusky haze that beckoned nighttime highlighted the white of her apron. He swallowed and bent to the work. When he had his hands full, he straightened.

"Bring them on over here to me."

His feet sunk into the soft earth. When he reached Marylu, her apron already pregnant with greens, he dropped the bundle into the snowy white cloth. He lifted his eyes to her face and studied the cheekbones lined by the lowering sun, the maple syrup of her eyes. The urge to kiss her pulled at him, yet he hesitated. Too late, she lowered her face.

"I'll leave the rest for now," she said and took a step back.

Chester's heart squeezed in his chest. He didn't move, and neither did she, but she didn't look at him either. He wondered if she had felt it too, that pull. The moon brightened and shone down stronger on her shoulders.

She gave him a furtive glance then leaned her head back to look up into the sky. "It's beautiful," Marylu whispered. "Makes me wonder if Miss Jenny is having a good time."

He didn't want to talk about Jenny or Cooper or Zedikiah. He wanted to tell her how her skin glowed with a subtle light and how her patience had grown his confidence. That her kind words swelled his courage and made him feel more worthy than he had felt in a long time. That though she discounted what she had done, she would always be a heroine to him. Driven by the deep longing of his heart, he lifted his hand and cupped her cheek. "You beautiful."

Her eyes glowed, and she did not look away as he'd feared she might. "Only one other person has told me that before."

He wasn't surprised by the revelation. "Tell me."

Her lower lip trembled. She could and would have looked away if he hadn't held her chin. It was obvious to him that what she was about to tell him was painful. He dropped his hand from her cheek and stroked down her arm, only to clasp her fingers and squeeze, willing his strength to be hers.

❧

She wanted so much not to cry. Walter was a long time ago and now she had this man standing in front of her, loving her, and all she could think about was *him*. It wasn't fair to Chester, yet something beckoned her to bare her heart to him as he had to her.

"His name was Walter." She swallowed hard. "He was one of the people we rescued that night. He got hurt in the rescue, and my ankle got busted. I cared for him for three months, and we fell in love." She paused and raised her eyes to the sky, dark and full of stars. "At least *I* fell in love," she whispered.

It pained her to say that, to admit it. And yet it felt so right to say those words to the man who had already declared his love for her. She felt his gentle squeeze on her fingers again and stared into his face, surprised to see the tears on his cheeks. How could she have ever thought this man, this gentle heart, could have murdered another man in cold blood?

"He left me. Said he had to move on while he could." She pressed her lips together. "But I couldn't move on."

With his free hand, Chester pointed to himself. "I no leave."

Her lips trembled, and she bit down hard on the lower one. Tears slid out from under her lids, and she squeezed her eyes tight, willing away the torrent that threatened. The soft pads of his thumbs wiped at the wetness on her cheeks. When she felt the palms of his hands press against the sides of her face, she opened her eyes.

"I'm not Walter." And with that he leaned forward and planted a warm kiss on her forehead.

A creaking sound broke the stillness surrounding them. "Marylu? Me and Zedikiah are awful hungry," Cooper croaked in a voice that probably carried halfway across the town.

Marylu blinked up at Chester. "I guess Zedikiah got him to help after all." She grinned. Then, softer, "We need to be going inside."

Chester looked down toward their feet and chuckled. She followed his gaze, not understanding what he found so funny until she realized all the greens lay in a heap at their feet. In all the emotion of the last few moments, she'd forgotten the greens and released her apron.

"Guess we'd best be picking more, or they might think—"

Chester's laugh barked out. "We kissing?"

Marylu ducked her head and made as if to kneel to collect the leaves, but his hand under her elbow pulled her upright. He put his arm around her shoulder and wheeled her around to face the back of the house. "I don't mind them thinking it. You?" The words came out so clear, so full of conviction. His eyes danced with the mischief he must have felt.

Her shyness melted away. "No. No, I don't mind a bit."

She popped through the doorway first, squinting against the bright lantern light. Cooper had resumed his seat, but she didn't miss his raised brow nor Zedikiah's inquisitive gaze.

"Got all these sorted," the boy said. "Thought you were bringing more."

Chester stepped through the door behind her, and she moved aside.

"Were. They got lost," Chester replied with a grin and a wink. When every eye fell on Marylu, it was more than she could take. She crossed to the cookstove and began stirring.

Zedikiah sidled up beside her and placed the basket of collards beside her and another basket of spinach beside that.

"You go wash up. Supper will be done soon."

Zedikiah nodded and relayed the message to the other men.

She got lost in the final preparations of supper and got everyone fed and the kitchen cleaned up in record time, her ear tuned in to the chatter of the men. As she put away the last plate, her mind buzzed about the minstrel show and Miss Jenny. What made her smile was the image of Sally's face when she set her eyes on Miss Jenny's dress. That should set her back on her heels.

Marylu set the dish towel aside and turned, colliding with a solid chest. Chester's hands clasped her upper arms as her hand groped for something solid to steady herself. She latched onto a chunk of his shirt front. Her cheeks heated, and she released him. "You enjoy flustering me," she shot at him.

His mouth curved upward for a second before he released her and stepped away.

"If I had my dish towel, I'd give you a good swat."

"If you two will stop your lovers' spat," Cooper groused, "we can read the Good Book."

Marylu sent Chester a mock frown and stepped around him. Chester settled down beside her, and she felt the same protected feeling she had felt on the wagon seat. His eyes were not on her, though, but on Cooper.

The old man's expression puzzled her, filled with an emotion she could not discern. It was as if the men warred on a level she could not understand. Cooper looked away first.

If Chester noticed anything amiss, he didn't let on and instead tugged the Bible across the table to himself. "Zed read Absalom and David." He flipped back a few pages. "Read about David's wrongs." He fastened his gaze on Cooper. "Father done wrong first. Hurt others."

Marylu wished she understood what was going on between Chester and Cooper. "David wronged Uriah." Was Chester referring to his friend betraying him again? She couldn't wrap her mind around what it had to do with Cooper, though.

Chester used his finger as he read. She leaned in close to see the verse highlighted by his finger and helped when he struggled to sound out the words of II Samuel 12:15. They took turns reading a scripture, until the Bible went to Cooper. He stumbled over the reading of the eighteenth verse and finally passed the Book back to Chester, the scripture unread.

"You getting sick again?" Marylu asked.

He shrugged and shot out a cough. "I'm fine, just not feeling much like reading."

She didn't believe Cooper for a minute, but something about the mulish glint in his eyes told her not to push. Marylu returned her attention to finishing up the Bible reading through the twenty-first verse. She motioned for Chester to pick up reading.

Zedikiah frowned as Chester finished reading verse twenty-five and closed the book.

"Makes me miss my mama awful bad."

"She want you be good man," Chester admonished in his slow, halting speech. "Work hard."

"It took David awhile to really see how much wrong he'd done," Marylu inserted.

"Did I do wrong?" Zedikiah asked. "Is that why He took my mama?"

Chester shook his head. "No. You young." He stared at Marylu with a pleading look.

"What I think Chester is meaning is this. You have to trust He wants what's best for you, and sometimes it means people we love die sooner than we want. We can learn other lessons then. How to grow up and be strong."

"Chester just found out his own mama died while he was away. Should he blame himself for her dying?"

Zedikiah stared down at his hands. Beside him, Cooper shifted and covered his face. Chester's gaze met Marylu's.

"No. I know lots of people who've died," Zedikiah finally answered.

"God comfort you. Make you strong. He be your God," Chester added.

Marylu nodded her agreement. "And we'll be your family."

The boy's brown eyes held the telltale sheen of tears, and Marylu stretched out her hand, palm up. Zedikiah clasped hers. A deep sob shattered the moment. Cooper's heaving shoulders told the tale.

Chester went to the man and braced a hand on his shoulder. "Cooper?"

But all that could be heard were the sharp intakes of breath, followed by shuddering sobs.

Beside the man, Zedikiah looked scared.

Marylu slipped her hand from his, her gaze bouncing from Chester's to Cooper.

Cooper moaned and rocked on the bench.

"Cooper?" Marylu bounced to her feet. "You're not sick, are you?"

Her only answer was deep, aching moans.

She swung her legs around and went to Cooper's side. "Here," she directed Chester. "You and Zedikiah lift him and lay him out right here."

"No," Cooper snapped and lifted his head. "Just let me be."

twenty-five

Chester touched Marylu's elbow and gave a sharp shake of his head. Surprised by the silent command, she stood for a minute as he crossed the room and flung open the door. He cast a look back at her that begged her to follow.

"This is becoming a habit. Slamming in and out," she said. The night air held a distinct chill that it hadn't an hour before. "What is it?" she asked as she crossed her arms and rubbed her skin to ward off the cold.

He faced her, eyes searching her face. "He loved you. Long time ago," Chester finished.

Marylu shifted her weight. "He told you that?"

He nodded.

Cooper had been in love with her? She set aside her confusion over the direction the conversation had taken and thought back over the years. Cooper had become a fixture in the McGreary household after being rescued off the wagon with the others. He had known Walter, and when Walter left, he had stayed. But love? She couldn't remember Cooper ever indicating love for her. Sure, they sparred and picked at each other. But love? She shook her head in answer.

Chester's eyes drilled into her. He seemed to be searching for the answer in her face the way his gaze raked over her. "Never fight?"

Restlessness crept over her. "You mean, did we ever fight?" Why wouldn't Chester just say outright what he was after? His tongue might be injured and his speech slow, but surely he knew she would hear him out. She pulled her gaze from his and skimmed along the ground, again pushing herself to remember something, anything.

She remembered once, about a year after Walter left, that

Cooper's mood had become surly and she'd gotten fed up with his biting answers and snappish comments. "If you can't say something nice, then get out of here. Take yourself on a long walk and don't come back until you're able to talk nice."

Cooper's eyes had sparked fire. "Maybe I will, and maybe I won't come back. Doesn't seem you'd notice either way."

Marylu recalled the way the back wall had shook from the force of the door slamming behind him. He hadn't returned for two full days and two full nights. She'd worried that the McGrearys would notice his absence and blame her. Only the then-young Jenny had asked about Cooper. Marylu had told her exactly what had happened and recalled how the young woman's eyes filled with tears.

But that had been a long time ago and the biggest argument she could recall having with Cooper.

"What?" Chester's voice urged. "You remember?"

She shrugged. "It was nothing. I told Cooper to leave one time until he could stop being so mean."

Chester's eyes widened. "You young then?"

Her exasperation rose. "What are you getting at? What does this have to do with anything?"

Chester reached out and captured her hand. His eyes begged her to understand. "Be patient."

Marylu heaved a breath. "I was young, yes, about a year after we got everyone out of that wagon."

"Tell me."

She bit down on her impatience and reviewed the incident before relaying it, verbatim, to Chester.

"That's it." Chester nodded and he released her hand, caught up in some mystery that she did not understand.

"But it was a long time ago. Surely he don't still love me now."

Chester licked his lips. "Maybe not. No matter."

"I don't understand. He loved me. Why does it matter now?"

"You not love him back. He left. Two nights." He paused, holding her gaze. "How old is Zedikiah?"

She processed the change in subject and how the two

might connect. Dottie, Zedikiah's mother, had come up pregnant. No father had ever been named, and Dottie had never said a word, though she always seemed interested in talking to Cooper when she got the chance. Marylu gasped. "Cooper is Zedikiah's daddy?"

Chester steadied her. "Makes sense. He cry earlier. Zedikiah talk about his daddy."

Her mind tripped along the new path of thinking Chester had paved. "It does make sense." And something else occurred to her. "Jenny. She knows something."

Chester drew his brows together in question.

"Her and Cooper have been keeping something secret. I'm sure of it. And it all came about as talk of Zedikiah's been coming up more and more." Marylu realized if it were true that Cooper had fathered Zedikiah, it had happened, in part, because of her. She closed her eyes and renewed her commitment to help the boy. "I didn't know how he felt, Chester. He never said a word. I mean, never *those* words."

Chester responded with a nod and a gentle caress against her cheek.

"Do you think he's telling Zedikiah right now? Is that why you left?"

"No. Not all."

❧

She had saved him again, and she didn't even know it. A trembling started in his chest, and he pushed aside thoughts of Cooper. What mattered to him now was God. His mama's God.

"You said Zed not blame for mama's death."

Marylu's lips parted. "Why, of course not." He felt her question as their eyes met. "Do you blame yourself?"

He had banked himself in the feeling that bad things happened to him because he somehow was not good enough. While some grew bitter, he had grown distant. But more than that, Marylu's statement to Zedikiah had pulled an answer from him that surprised him. "I always thought God was for my mama. Her God." He swallowed, wondering if she understood what he meant.

"He is your God, too. He can be if you open your heart to Him."

For so long he had thought his religion sufficient. He'd gone to the little church in the South because his mama had gone. It always felt right somehow because he knew his mama's faith was real and figured his would be, too. But it wasn't, he realized. Even over his mama's grave, he had known something was missing from his heart. He understood now. It was as he had said to Zedikiah, "He'll be your God."

Tears rushed down his cheeks.

Marylu held out her hand. "Chester?"

"Want Him." He pulled in a shuddering breath. "In here." He stabbed at his chest then brushed the wetness from his cheeks. He didn't know what to do, so he did what he had seen his mama do. He got down on his knees.

Marylu knelt beside him, her tears mingled with his.

twenty-six

They walked back toward the house hand-in-hand, spent and exhausted, yet Marylu felt flush with the victory Chester had won. The kitchen remained well lit, and Zedikiah sat at the table alone. The sight of the young man squeezed Marylu's heart anew. "You set yourself down, Chester, and I'll serve up some apple cake."

Zedikiah raised his head. A small smile teased along the edges of his mouth. Chester emphasized his approval by rubbing his stomach. He chose the spot next to Zedikiah that Cooper had vacated at some point. They spoke in low tones, Chester's responses short and slow, Zedikiah's longer and more drawn out.

She cut generous slices of the cake and breathed a prayer for Cooper. If what Chester suspected was true, how could the man have denied his own son? Zedikiah's drunken binges had gone on for months. If Cooper had stepped in after Dottie's death, he could have prevented much of the boy's wildness. She considered the dull edge of the knife in her hand and considered how hard it would be to penetrate the tough hide of Cooper's conscience. And here he had sat, night after night, listening to God's Word and never letting on.

How was she to know he'd go off and do something so irresponsible? And if she had known, would it have made a difference? Cooper was too old for her now and had been too old for her then.

She set the dishes in front of the men and stared at the clock over their heads. Maybe she should check on Cooper, but no, she was too angry. She decided the best use of her time would be to work with Chester on his reading and speech.

They worked for another hour, with Zedikiah getting into the methods she used to show Chester how to work his tongue. When the front door opened, her concentration shattered. Chester caught her eye, darted a glance at Zedikiah, and then gave her a meaningful look.

She rose from the table with a smile at Zedikiah. "Why don't you work with Chester while I go check on Miss Jenny?"

❧

As Zedikiah and Chester worked over the slate, Chester's mind worked on another level entirely. The boy had a gift for teaching and seemed to know quite a bit. Probably something unknown to most since he spent most of his nights drunk and a good portion of his days in a drunken stupor. He'd put on weight since eating Marylu's cooking and had begun to lose the sickly hollowness beneath his cheeks.

Chester saw himself in the boy. Lost. No one to guide him along the way, resulting in an indifference to people, and to life and all that it entailed. As Zedikiah looked through the Bible for a passage to work on Chester's reading, he felt a stirring in his spirit. Ruth's admonition to go and make a life for himself joined with the stirring and swelled. This would be his life. Marylu. Zedikiah. Cooper, if the man would allow. Perhaps even Miss Jenny, if she welcomed him into the circle.

Zedikiah pointed to a verse. "Read this."

Chester glanced at the chapter. Luke. He began, stumbling over the harder words but taking Zedikiah's gentle correction and forging ahead. As if from a great distance, he heard the same words falling from the lips of his mother when he was but a child. A Samaritan man who showed mercy to a stranger when other men passed the stranger by without more than a glance.

Zedikiah was that stranger, just as he, himself, had been a stranger before this night, kneeling in the grass beside Marylu. God had brought him back from his wanderings and shown him mercy when all else had failed him. He was to show Zedikiah. Tend to his physical needs and spiritual.

He left after reading the passage, the voices of the women assuring him they had much to talk about and Zedikiah's exhaustion visible in his face. Chester wrestled with the hows of doing what he felt led to do. Zedikiah wasn't his son. He could show the young man some things, but he could not take the place of his real father.

It didn't matter, though, he supposed. God would show him what to do one day at a time.

&

Marylu heard the men moving around in the kitchen but felt compelled to stay and listen to Jenny's excited chatter about the show. What could have been a dismal evening for her friend had turned into a wonderful experience.

"Then he sang another song, and his voice brought everyone to their feet." Jenny rubbed a hand over her forearm. "It gave me goose pimples to hear him. Oh, I wish you would have come."

"Maybe next time me and Chester will go along. Did you see Mr. Walck and Sally again?"

Jenny nodded. "Abigail Cross made sure to point them out as we made our exit." A faraway look came into her eyes. "They didn't appear very excited to be together. Nothing like the excitement Sally showed at the store."

Marylu wondered if it had anything to do with her visit to Aaron Walck. Good, maybe it had begun to sink in. He was headed for a heap of trouble with Sally clinging to him.

Jenny stretched and covered a huge yawn. "I'll be asleep in no time."

She moved as if to rise, but Marylu caught the material of her skirt and gave a light tug. "There's something I need to ask you."

"Ask away."

"Might want to be sitting."

Jenny sat back down on the chair she'd just vacated. "Now you've got me curious."

Marylu gathered her thoughts and rolled right into the

subject. "Cooper's been acting strange. Tonight he started sobbing when we were reading the Word."

"Is he not feeling well?"

"Right as rain. But troubled."

Jenny's expression became grave. "And you think I know what's wrong with him."

Marylu noted that it wasn't a question but a statement. "I haven't missed how the two of you keep communicating with each other in a way that excludes me."

Jenny stared down at her hands. "Was Zedikiah there when you were reading?"

Her heart stumbled and picked up speed. "Sitting right across from Cooper."

A little sigh escaped Jenny's lips. "It's not my secret to tell, Marylu. I promised Cooper I'd be quiet about it, and I can't go back on my word."

Marylu understood the position it put Jenny in and tried another angle. "It seems ridiculous, but Chester is convinced that Cooper was in love with me years ago. Around the time Walter was here."

If she expected Jenny to smile and laugh, it didn't happen. Her friend's reaction solidified Chester's assumption. "I've always known it. The way he watched you and talked about you, but you never seemed to care. He told me one night that your heroism had elevated you to a level he could never hope to reach."

Deep in her stomach, something fisted and froze. "That's plain nonsense. I never acted different. Never took to all those who called me Queenie." Marylu cast about for some explanation. Why would her friend think such a thing?

"I've always thought it was your hurt over Walter that made him feel that way. You were pretty distant after he left."

"You know why."

"Yes"—Jenny reached out to clasp her hand—"I understood that, but. . ." She pressed her lips together. "Let's let Cooper explain."

❧

Chester stretched and greeted the blue sky. A lone wagon bobbled down the street in front of the hotel, driven by a man encouraging a horse that seemed disinterested in arriving anywhere, at anytime. The sight brought a smile to Chester's lips.

He went north on Washington Street and took a left onto Madison. In the distance, he made out the form of another man headed his way and realized it was Zedikiah. The boy had made it through another night sober. He rejoiced in his heart for the accomplishment and, as they pulled even with each other, offered his hand.

Zedikiah slapped his palm against Chester's, but no smile appeared on his lips.

"Ate Marylu's breakfast, and you're frowning?"

The young man paused before replying, and Chester knew it took him a moment to make out some of the blurrier words he'd spoken aloud. "Mighty good cook, that one. Miss Jenny made biscuits that'll make you miss your mama."

Chester nodded and felt a stir of sadness. "Not hard to miss my mama."

Zedikiah winced.

Chester wanted to ask so much more, to sit down with the young man and talk him through the grief and disappointment, but his hesitant speech held him back.

Zedikiah lowered his head and started down Madison, retracing the steps Chester had just taken.

He let the boy go. They could talk later, when it wouldn't risk Zedikiah being late for work.

As soon as Chester set foot into the kitchen, Marylu slid a plate, heaped with biscuits, butter, and gravy, in front of him.

"Been expecting you." She smiled into his eyes.

He leaned toward her so Miss Jenny wouldn't hear. "Miss me?"

Marylu laughed and swatted at him, casting a wary eye over at her friend, but Miss Jenny didn't seem to notice them at all. "She probably got her head in the clouds over last night's doings."

He slipped onto the bench and pulled the steaming plate of food toward him. "Where's Cooper?"

Miss Jenny turned at that. She shared a look with Marylu, who finally looked back at him and shrugged. "Still sleeping." Marylu set a cup of coffee in front of him. "What you going to do now that you don't have work?"

Chester winked at her and waggled his brows. To his delight, she looked abashed.

Miss Jenny crossed to the table and joined them as Chester stabbed his fork into a piece of biscuit.

Marylu passed Jenny a plate with a biscuit. "Marylu told me you gave up your job for Zedikiah. Did you check down at the railroad?"

Chester bobbed his head and took a small sip of the hot coffee so he wouldn't embarrass himself if it was too hot. He found it easier to handle liquids since he'd been working his tongue more and more. Guessed it was getting stronger after all. "Wanted to work for you," he said to Miss Jenny but, realizing how it sounded, rushed to add, "pay for my meals."

Miss Jenny's soft smile spilled over him. "No need for that, Chester. You're welcome at this table any time. Any day."

"Sure could use help taking up greens, though," Marylu added, a twinkle in her eyes.

Jenny stared at her friend, obviously confused. "You could ask Cooper to help you. Or Zedikiah."

Chester guffawed, and Jenny pursed her lips, her gaze darting between him and Marylu. "I'm guessing this is a secret joke of some sort?"

Marylu joined them at the table. "What I've been wondering is what we're going to do with Zedikiah. Him sleeping over at the hotel means we can't keep an eye on him, and Cooper's place is hardly big enough for *him.*"

It was the dilemma Chester had struggled with as well.

Miss Jenny's eyes scanned the kitchen, the doorway that

led to the rooms downstairs, and then back to Marylu. "He needs a space of his own."

Chester latched onto the idea. He set his fork aside. "Zedikiah"—he held up a finger—"Marylu"—another finger—"Cooper"—and then the third finger went up—"and Miss Jenny. But three rooms."

"*You* need a place to stay," Marylu reminded him.

He shook his head. "I find somewhere."

"What about the shop?" Miss Jenny brightened. "You and Zedikiah can stay there. There's that big back room that we use for storage, but I think it could be turned into a decent bedroom."

"I work for place," he said, then folded his hands and lay his head against them to indicate he meant a place to sleep. It would work though, he knew. He could keep an eye on Zedikiah, and the boy could help him with his reading and speech.

"And I'll feed us all up real good." Marylu threw out the offer, her expression showing her deep satisfaction at the prospect.

Chester beamed at her, his heart full.

❧

Underlying her happiness, Marylu felt concern for Cooper and Zedikiah. The old man never did come out of his room to eat. At her insistence, Miss Jenny had knocked on his door to make sure he was fine. But Zedikiah, too, had seemed sad, and Marylu hoped it didn't mean the boy was going to seek out the only comfort he'd known for all these years.

As Miss Jenny worked a beautiful blue silk through the sewing machine at the dress shop and Chester worked on hammering together a wall to separate the storage room into two rooms, Marylu put her worry to words. "If that Cooper doesn't show himself tonight, I'm going to drag him out of there."

Jenny's foot stopped pedaling the machine. "Where did that come from?"

Marylu opened her mouth, then pressed her hand to her lips and swallowed hard over the lump there. Through the night and all morning she had dodged the guilt, but now, with the afternoon settling into a slower pace, it came rushing down on her. "I just wish I'd known. Maybe. . ."

Jenny must have sensed her despair, for she stood and came to her. "Cooper made his choice, Marylu. And I'm sure he will talk to us, but give him some time. I think the Lord is dealing with him."

It took Marylu by surprise, but it made sense. Between Cooper's sickness and his strange behavior of late, God's hand and timing had to be acknowledged and respected.

The door to the shop opened, and Marylu raised her head to see Aaron Walck come through.

Behind her, Jenny did a little gasp. She slipped out from behind Marylu and approached the man as she would any other customer. "Can I help you?"

"Yes." His eyes skipped over her face then away. "I—I—" He stared at Marylu a minute.

She nodded at him and raised her brows.

A small smile tugged at his lips, and he inclined his head, cleared his throat, and locked his gaze on Jenny. "I came to talk to you, Miss McGreary."

Chester ambled into the room, holding a fistful of nails, a question in his eyes. When he saw Aaron and Jenny, his mouth curved into a small smile.

Marylu placed a finger against his lips and backed him toward the storage room.

He grinned down at her. "Miss Jenny have caller?"

"Yes, and I'm not about to let you go out there and ask her a question about boards or nails or anything else to mess up what he's come to do."

Chester arched an eyebrow at her. "What he come to do? You know something?"

Marylu ducked her head and wondered how it was the man could so easily read her. It was at once troubling and reassuring. "She's loved him for a long time."

"Widower?"

"Yes. But another woman had her eye on him." She explained about Sally and her own visit to Aaron's store.

Chester chuckled and shook his head.

She pounded him on the arm. "I don't want her to be lonely anymore."

Something shifted in his expression. His gaze went intense. His hand came up to cup her chin. "I don't want to be lonely."

Her heart tripped, and a song rose to her lips that had nothing to do with music or words but joy. Caught in the light of his warm gaze, she shivered and gave her head a little shake. "I don't want to be either."

"Will you be my woman?"

Marylu stiffened, cautious about his use of the term *woman*.

Chester chuckled and pressed his thumb against her lips. "My queen?"

She drew air into her lungs and held her breath as he opened his mouth again.

"My wife?"

twenty-seven

Two skillets, filled with lard, popped and spattered as the batter for doughnuts hit the hot grease. The two women grinned at each other as the implication of the skillets and the hot grease dawned on both of them.

"And I thought you said you'd never pop and spatter like hot grease in a skillet." Jenny's eyes twinkled.

"Seems to me you're spattering, too."

Jenny chuckled. "I can't believe it, Marylu." She put another spoonful of lard into each skillet. "Are you sure you can handle that dress order by yourself Tuesday night?"

It had been a question Jenny had asked three times. "I'm sure as that grease popping."

They burst into giggles.

"Won't they be surprised to find doughnuts for dessert?" Jenny asked. "Do you think it was too forward of me to ask him over for supper tonight?"

"It wasn't your idea. It was mine. Chester said Mr. Walck looked surprised but excited. Probably sick of his own cooking." Marylu ducked to see out the kitchen window. The sun had long ago sunk toward the west, but enough light still lit the sky for her to be able to see into the backyard. No sign of anyone headed toward the door. "I hope Zedikiah gets here soon."

"Chester will probably think to swing by and check in on him. Seems he should have been back from Mr. Walck's shop long before now."

Marylu took down the tin of cinnamon and put two pinches of the spice into the batter. "They did seem to take to each other." She secretly hoped that Mr. Walck would offer Chester a job.

"Aaron—" Jenny's gaze darted to Marylu's. A blush crept over the woman's cheeks. "I mean, Mr. Walck." She cleared her throat and busied herself with gathering plates. "I think he was impressed with Chester's knowledge of wood."

Mr. Walck's departure from the shop had led to a flurry of words and excited squeals between the two women. Jenny had shared the reason for their visitor's appearance. "He told Sally he didn't think it would work out between them and that he couldn't put me out of his mind."

The news swelled Marylu's heart to bursting, and when she told Jenny that Chester had proposed, Jenny wanted all the details. They had chattered throughout the afternoon, even rejoicing over an order for a trousseau that meant steady work.

Marylu sprinkled a light coating of flour on the work surface and began to roll out the dough. "Grease ready?"

Together they made short work of frying the doughnuts. A platter of golden rounds, sprinkled with cinnamon sugar, sat on the table, dead center. Marylu frowned at the door and checked on the chicken she had baked. "If those men don't get here soon, that chicken's going to be tough as an old rooster."

Wagon wheels rattled, and Marylu and Jenny both stilled to listen close. Marylu swung the back door open and squinted into the growing darkness. "No use guessing when we can look for ourselves." But when her eyes adjusted, she saw the wagon pull up and Mr. Walck and Chester helping down a wobbling Zedikiah. "Oh no."

Jenny hurried up beside her, glanced at the situation, then turned and stared at the table. "Where do we put him?"

"He can't lay out on the floor. Put him in my room," Marylu urged the men as they neared. The smell of alcohol was heavy on Zedikiah.

Miss Jenny's nose wrinkled.

Marylu led the way to her room. They settled Zedikiah down onto the bed.

Chester pulled his feet up. He looked at Marylu with

sorrowful eyes. "Shouldn't have left him alone."

She recognized his agony, as it mirrored her own spirit. Even though she thought of Zedikiah as a boy, she knew he was a man by most standards. His drinking would destroy him, as she had seen it destroy countless others. "All we can do is pray and keep an eye on him. Does Mr. Shillito know about this?"

Chester nodded, and Mr. Walck spoke up for the first time. "It's why we were late. Apparently Zedikiah left early, before he'd taken care of some repairs on the sagging overhang that the buggies park under to unload. Chester and I stayed to finish up the project."

"Is Mr. Shillito going to fire him?"

Chester shook his head. "No. We told him"—he lifted his hand as if it held a bottle—"that we try to help him."

"He was kind about the situation," Mr. Walck assured. "But we assured Shillito that if he'd give Zedikiah the chance, we would help out should he go out on a binge again. I think he wanted to help the boy as much as we do."

Touched by Aaron's inclusion and Mr. Shillito's compassion, Marylu turned and swallowed to ease the ache in her throat. "Sure appreciate it. Let me get you some coffee."

When Marylu felt her wrist enclosed by a hand, she turned to see Chester's eyes begging her to wait. She caught Mr. Walck's gaze. "You go on ahead to the kitchen. Miss Jenny's in there and most likely got a pot boiling."

❧

Chester berated himself over and over for not talking to Zedikiah that morning. Surely the boy would have opened up about whatever it was that troubled him. As Mr. Walck left him alone with Marylu, he knew what he was about to demand would place a great strain on the household that had taken him in, but his conscience told him he had no choice. "Cooper?" he put the question to Marylu.

"He's not come out all morning."

He tugged on her wrist. "Talk to him."

Marylu stiffened. "I don't know. Shouldn't we wait until he's ready to talk? Miss Jenny thought the Lord might be dealing with him."

Chester shot a look over at the unconscious Zedikiah then back to her. *Lord, what do I do?*

It had become a rote prayer offered up when they found Zedikiah drunk, then again and again as they finished up the work and brought the boy to Jenny's house. It had been easy to blame himself. For a minute, his senses flared with the remembered scent of rain and wet fields. His mind flashed to the image of cotton, rows and rows, all edged by woods. He could feel the grip of Samuel's hands holding one of his arms and Old Bob the other. A light breeze ruffled the shirt, rent beneath the whipping he'd endured, edges encrusted in blood.

He had been made to kneel for this. The final punishment. His master stood over him, knife poised. Samuel had been the one to hold his jaws open as the master, blade in hand, had worked the edge under his tongue. His muscles had bunched, and his arms strained, and he knew he could not let them do this to him. As the blade began the slice, something inside his head had exploded. With a heave, he butted his head upward, into his persecutor's jaw. The master had fallen backward, his head dashed against a large boulder. Samuel and Old Bob were both thrown aside by the force of his upward thrust. He stood over the white man and watched the blood trickle from his mouth. The paleness of the face gone even more pale.

And then the voice. Samuel's. "Look what you done. You better run. Better run hard and fast and hope no one ever catches you for killing the master."

Chester had done just that. Terrified. Fearful of getting caught and put to death. Of hanging. He had run far and hidden himself. Then the lies had begun. Covering his true identity. Cowering in the shadows as law officers closed in.

He felt now as he had felt then. Helpless. Fearful. But this time he felt those traits for a person other than himself.

"Chester?" Marylu's hand tugged at his shirt.

He made a motion toward the door. "Let's see Cooper." Whatever else he was, he would not allow Zedikiah to wallow in his grief. Cooper held the key. He felt it deep inside his spirit.

twenty-eight

Cooper's eyes were swollen almost shut. From crying, by the looks of things. Jenny poured him a cup of hot coffee where he slumped at the end of the familiar kitchen table. It had surprised Marylu that Cooper insisted on having everyone present, as if he knew what was coming and wanted to make things right with everyone present as witnesses.

Cooper started slowly, as if his tongue were heavy and his mind slow. "Miss Jenny has wanted me to tell the truth for a long time. Months." He lifted his head and raised his brows. "I don't know how she found out, but I know it's created a misery in my soul for longer than I want to admit."

Chester ran his finger around the rim of his mug. Next to him, Aaron Walck sipped his coffee and nibbled on half a doughnut. Miss Jenny sat across from him, her gaze fixed on Cooper.

Marylu nudged the plate of doughnuts closer to Chester, encouraging him to eat, but he shook his head. She knew the feeling. Dread filled her stomach, leaving no room for appetite.

"You loved Marylu," Miss Jenny prodded the man.

Cooper nodded, a quirky smile on his lips. "She was the hero. Beautiful. Generous and brave. Most the men I know loved her. Even old Russell had himself a soft spot for her. But she never saw any of us. Except Walter." He pulled in a quick breath and lowered his eyes to the table.

"If only you'd said something," Marylu said.

Cooper laughed. "In your eyes I was an old man. Still am. I was chasing a fool's dream, and part of me knew it. Then I had to watch you and Walter, night after night." His head drooped forward. "It was me that told Walter to leave."

Marylu gasped and felt Miss Jenny's soft hand cup hers.

"I'd saved up a little bit working at Crowell and Davison as he healed up. It was all I had, and I gave it to him and told him to leave and get north. Forget about Marylu. That I would take care of her."

Quick anger stiffened Marylu's back. She wanted to shout a thousand things at Cooper, but only one slipped out. "How could you?"

Cooper didn't meet her eyes. "When you cried after him all those months, I couldn't take it anymore. So I. . ."

The wave of her emotion eased and morphed into resignation. It was a long time ago. Walter's love for her must have been very shallow indeed if he so easily was bought. She pulled in a deep, steadying breath.

"When you didn't love me back, I got mad. Went over to the widow's house. Dottie's." He ducked his head low between his extended arms, and the sounds of his heavy inhalation could be heard. "Zedikiah's my boy." The words came out, at once harsh and feeble. "Been burning a hole in me for a long time. Seeing him take to drink. I knew his mama would hate me for clamming up about being his daddy, but I didn't know how to go about being one, and he's already grown."

"He needs you," Chester said simply.

Cooper bobbed his head once. "I see that now. Don't mean I know what I'm doing, but it's right for me to tell him." He swallowed. "Maybe he'll hate me."

For the first time, Marylu felt his fear, as if it had been Walter leaving her all over again. She pressed her face into her hands and let the emotions burst forth. Cooper's betrayal. His deceit. Where hate should have been stirred to new heights, she could only feel a dull ache. What had happened happened a long time ago. If things hadn't occurred as they had, she might be saddled with a man she would have grown to hate. God only knew.

But was her love so easy to reject?

"Marylu?" Cooper's voice invaded her thoughts. When she raised her head and saw the veil of unshed tears clouding his eyes, she knew it was within her power to ease the man's burden. God would want her to do that. Still, the words came hard, but forgiveness, she knew, boiled down to choice. *Lord, I want to forgive him.* "I do love you, Cooper. You've been one of my best friends. You and Miss Jenny and her parents."

Cooper's shoulders quaked, and like a building made of sticks, his torso seemed to collapse into a heaving mass. His sobs filled the room.

Miss Jenny rose and went to the man. "It's all right, Cooper."

❧

The evening stretched long, the plate of doughnuts finally empty, polished off mostly by Chester and Aaron Walck. It filled Marylu with a quiet joy to see Mr. Walck staying close to Miss Jenny during the meal. When the man finally said his good-byes, Jenny blushed beneath his beaming smile. Her friend seemed wreathed in happiness despite the hard issue of Cooper's confession.

They waited for the moment when Zedikiah would awake and Cooper would spill his news. Marylu urged Cooper to reveal his relationship to Zedikiah in private, but Jenny argued that it might be better if it was done with everyone who loved the two men surrounding them.

Chester grabbed Marylu's hand and pointed to the door. "Go for walk."

She joined him in the cool night air, feeling a strange unreality about her surroundings. Mixed up in her mind less about her choice to forgive Cooper than about her fear that love wasn't meant for her. If Walter left so easily. . .

She cast a sidelong glance at Chester. Perhaps she was a foolish woman for thinking it wouldn't happen again, for allowing herself to marry a man who had left her once already.

Jenny's admonition shot through her mind. She could not let Walter's betrayal shadow what she had with Chester. And hadn't it been Chester who reminded her that he was not Walter?

It was too much, and her head ached with the weariness of suppressed emotion and confusion. She stopped in the middle of the walk, pulling her hand out of Chester's.

He turned toward her and took a step closer. She saw the question lurking in his eyes. "Tired?"

Such a simple question. Answering yes would be a way out, and she could retreat to the quiet of her room to sort through her feelings. "Very tired."

His eyes became searching, and she looked away. "We should head back." She turned away from him, giving movement to her suggestion, and saw his hand reach for hers. She raised her hand to touch her hair to avoid his contact, afraid she would shatter, fearful it meant putting her heart in danger all the more.

When he came even with her, she darted a quick look at him. His bowed head. Hands jammed in his pockets. Her heart ached with the dejection of his silhouette. In order not to be hurt, she hurt in return. Was that fair?

Before they got back to the back door of Miss Jenny's house, his words stopped her.

"I go Mercersburg."

Coldness froze her heart, and her gaze flew to his, but his eyes were in shadow. It burgeoned then, all the weariness and questions.

"I love you."

Emotion balled in her throat. Walter's last "I love you." Would she ever be able to trust those words? Marylu spun around and hurried to the house, ignoring Chester's throaty command to stop. And when she shut the door behind her, she waited for his knock. Hoping he might follow her, and dreading it if he did.

There was no knock.

Zedikiah and Cooper looked up from the table.

Jenny hurried to her. "Marylu?" Her cool hand on Marylu's arm brought an uncontrollable trembling to Marylu's limbs. "Sit down," Jenny directed.

By some unspoken agreement, Cooper disappeared in one direction, Zedikiah the other.

Marylu shook her head when Jenny tried to get her to talk. "Nothing to say."

"Marylu, that's not true, and you know it."

She laid eyes on Jenny's concerned expression. "I was right, Miss Jenny. No one can love me."

❧

Chester stretched out on the floor of Zedikiah's room. The boy had said little since he'd entered, and he guessed that Cooper's revelation had not resulted in warm feelings between them.

As his body relaxed, he thought of Marylu. He didn't think her shrinking away from him had anything to do with him, not in light of all that Cooper had revealed. His love for the woman must have been deep, though selfish. Chester admired her ability to forgive her old friend so easily, but something gnawed at her in spite of the gesture.

He hadn't known what to say, what with his tongue still not able to speak the volumes that lay dormant in his heart. And his timing in announcing his trip to Mercersburg seemed to startle her, but his nephew needed some help, and he would not say no to the boy or his sister. It had been his hope that Marylu would go with him and meet his family, but her taking off as she had left him little choice but to go alone.

Chester closed his eyes and prayed for Marylu and Zedikiah, Cooper and Miss Jenny, even Aaron Walck. But his mind took little rest from the prayer, and he slept restlessly. When he opened his eyes and darkness came through the window, he raised himself on one elbow and ran his hand over his face. He had almost convinced himself of the merit of starting out on the long walk to Mercersburg now, when he heard a sniffle. Then another.

"Zed?"

"Thought you was asleep."

"Was."

As his eyes adjusted to the dim light, Chester could make out the boy's form where he sat on the edge of the bed. He hiked up from the floor and crossed to the young man, placing a hand on his shoulder. "Talk?"

"Nothing to say."

Chester smiled in the darkness, seeing that there was plenty the boy wanted to say, but he just didn't want to form the words. Or didn't know what words to say. It all reminded him so much of himself. Zedikiah's habit of sliding into self-pity mirrored his own past tendencies to do the same. And it always led to drinking.

"Lord worked in his heart." Chester paused. "Got to let the past go. Look forward."

Zedikiah sat still, an occasional sniff the only sound in the room. "Is it that easy?"

Chester got to his feet, grabbed his shirt off a peg on the wall and shrugged into it. The answer to that question seemed riddled with pitfalls. For someone who couldn't see the answer for what it was, the choice to look forward would be difficult. He had tried for years himself, but once he had embraced the forgiveness and peace, he was able to heal. "Can be," he said.

Zedikiah lay back down on the bed and sighed. "Is that what you did?"

Chester stood straight, fingertips working the last button-hole. He smiled, knowing Zedikiah wouldn't be able to see it in the semidarkness, but it wasn't a smile for Zedikiah. It was one for himself. Proof of his victory. "Yes. And it works. God will help. Let Him."

"I'm not much for church." Zedikiah put his hand on the door and swung it inward.

"Can change that, too."

twenty-nine

In the morning light, Marylu pulled the thick strips of bacon from the skillet.

Cooper sat huddled on the bench, a miserable knot of a man. Jenny, dressed for Sunday church, sat across from him, speaking in low tones.

Marylu set the tin of bacon on the table.

Cooper didn't even raise his face, and when she exchanged a look with Jenny, her friend looked sad beyond words.

"Someone better be eating up this bacon."

"It smells wonderful," Jenny said out loud, her eyes on Cooper.

Without ever looking up, Cooper rose from the table and ambled out the back door.

"He is the most stubborn man," Jenny groused.

"You just now seeing that?"

Jenny nibbled on the bacon and a piece of dry toast before she pushed her plate away. "I'm just not hungry, Marylu."

"Going to see Mr. Walck this morning?"

"Of course. He is always faithful to the services. He sings, too." Twin spots of color showed on the woman's cheeks, and her eyes shone. Her smile faded, though, and Marylu knew what was coming. "I'm sorry about Cooper."

"It's not your fault."

"And what he did isn't your fault either."

Marylu eyed her friend. She let the words sink in, understanding exactly what Jenny meant.

"You wouldn't talk last night, but I figured I knew what was going through your mind. The way you came into the kitchen and how we never saw Chester after that."

Marylu pulled air into her lungs and stared down at the table.

"It's just like you somehow figured you weren't enough for Walter and that's why he left you. And with Cooper's confession, you did something of the same thing."

"He said he was going to Mercersburg."

Jenny tilted her head. "Chester?"

She nodded. "I felt so exhausted, and I guess. . . I guess I let my emotions and fears rattle me."

"He's probably going to see his sister. He got a note from her yesterday at the shop. I gave it to him."

Marylu closed her eyes.

"You thought he meant he was leaving? After he proposed?"

She shrugged.

"Marylu." Jenny's tone held reprimand. She rose from the table. "I guess I'll be walking to church this morning."

"Cooper's probably got the buggy ready."

Jenny shook her head. "No, I'll walk. Seems like that buggy will be headed west this morning. Don't you think?"

She laughed at her friend's less-than-subtle suggestion. "Seems I've done this once before."

"And both times for the right reasons."

☙

Finding Chester didn't take long. He had just made it within sight of Mercersburg when she pulled up beside him. His eyes widened with surprise.

"If you get in, I'll take you into Mercersburg."

The buggy rocked under his weight then settled when he sat beside her. He caught her gaze and held it, his brows raised.

She saw what he was asking. "I'm sorry. I was tired and confused and. . ." She bit down hard to keep from crying.

His hand covered hers.

"When you told me you were coming here, I didn't understand."

"I'm not Walter."

She gave a short laugh. "Yes, I know that. It's me. I just don't want to be hurt again."

He squeezed her fingers, and she raised her face to see the tenderness there in his eyes.

"I not Cooper." He placed a hand over his heart. "I love because you are dear, kind, devoted. You helped heal me. Showed me God."

Tears gathered in her eyes and blurred his features. She blinked and would have turned away, but he tugged on her hand.

"You make me better man. I need you."

She drew in a shuddering breath. "All this time I thought Walter had left me because I wasn't loveable, but now I know that it was Cooper's doing. I don't know. It's like I can't help but be thankful. What kind of man would say he loves me then leave so easily?"

Chester's face remained expressionless.

"Not the kind I want to share my life with, I'll tell you that. It's like God was watching over me the entire time. Answering my prayers even though my heart was breaking." She stopped and stared out over the fields.

All those prayers. All the tears. Yet God had seen them all and bided time in order to bring Chester to her. She turned back toward him and scanned his gentle face, the wrinkles set around his dark eyes, and she knew in her heart that she could love again. Wholly. And that she did love. The wonder of it settled over her shoulders and deep into her heart. She squeezed his fingers until a smile lit his face.

He pulled her hand to his lips and pressed a gentle kiss against her skin.

She leaned toward him and tilted her head up, giving him a saucy smile.

He didn't move.

"Don't you know an invitation for a kiss when you see one?" She breathed.

His smile came slowly. He leaned in toward her and bowed his head over hers until she felt the warmth of his lips.

In that moment, Marylu Biloxi decided popping and crackling over a man wasn't such a bad thing after all.

epilogue

Chester was my husband for thirty-two years. The good Lord added him to his collection of saints on a cool, autumn day when the leaves were just beginning to fall from the trees. I rejoiced in his rest, being that he had suffered much after a stroke left him weak on his right side and robbed him of his ability to walk. I'm more sure than anything that he's bouncing all over heaven though. We had a good life together. It seemed once we'd cleansed ourselves of all the demons of our youth that life became sweeter. Even more so because it was shared by us together.

We had us a couple of little surprises along the way. Lillian Jennifer Jones was born right after my thirty-second birthday. Our next little one died, a little boy we called William, and was laid in the cemetery with many tears. On my thirty-seventh birthday, I found myself with child again. This boy came into the world screaming for all he was worth and never stopped. Chester Jones, Jr., was our crowning glory, though he about near killed us both with his wild ways before finally settling down at the age of seventeen.

Miss Jenny and Aaron Walck married shortly after me and Chester. They had a whole passel of young ones. Six babies, one almost right after the other. It wore her out, having all those babies close together, which made it a good thing that Chester and me lived in a little cabin right out back of Aaron's home. It was like caring for Miss Jenny all over again.

And Zedikiah? He had a hard road. We worked together to care for him as best we could. After a rough start, he finally settled down in his work and eventually he became Aaron Walck's most trusted craftsman. Cooper played a minor role in his life, I'm sorry to say. Zedikiah never quite took to having him for a father.

I'm guessing that sometimes we only get one chance to set things right. Cooper had his chance, and though he cleared his conscience by confessing to Zedikiah, he was never quite able to move beyond the fact that had he made things right sooner, things would have been different. Both for him and Zedikiah.

Still, he died in his son's arms, and Zedikiah visited his grave often. Sad to see. Best to heal rifts when you're alive than after someone is dead and gone. But the world isn't a perfect place, and people aren't perfect either. Only God is perfect. It's up to us to be more like Him, but some come to it later than others, and some not at all.

I lay my pen aside now, hoping that someone might read this love story and realize that you don't have to be young to find true love. Sometimes it's even better to be older, because youthful longings can choose the wrong person.

My heart is content to leave you in His care.

Marylu Jones
December, 1915

A Letter To Our Readers

Dear Reader:

In order that we might better contribute to your reading enjoyment, we would appreciate your taking a few minutes to respond to the following questions. We welcome your comments and read each form and letter we receive. When completed, please return to the following:

Fiction Editor
Heartsong Presents
PO Box 719
Uhrichsville, Ohio 44683

1. Did you enjoy reading *Promise of Yesterday* by S. Dionne Moore?
   ❑ Very much! I would like to see more books by this author!
   ❑ Moderately. I would have enjoyed it more if

   _____

   _____

   _____

2. Are you a member of **Heartsong Presents**? ❑ Yes ❑ No
   If no, where did you purchase this book? _____

   _____

3. How would you rate, on a scale from 1 (poor) to 5 (superior), the cover design? _____

4. On a scale from 1 (poor) to 10 (superior), please rate the following elements.

   ____ Heroine   ____ Plot
   ____ Hero   ____ Inspirational theme
   ____ Setting   ____ Secondary characters

5. These characters were special because? _____

_____

_____

6. How has this book inspired your life? _____

_____

_____

7. What settings would you like to see covered in future
   Heartsong Presents books? _____

_____

_____

8. What are some inspirational themes you would like to see
   treated in future books? _____

_____

_____

9. Would you be interested in reading other **Heartsong
   Presents** titles? ❏ Yes ❏ No

10. Please check your age range:
   ❏ Under 18   ❏ 18-24
   ❏ 25-34   ❏ 35-45
   ❏ 46-55   ❏ Over 55

Name _____

Occupation _____

Address _____

City, State, Zip_____

E-mail _____

WINDY CITY BRIDES

The couples rely on faith and love to get them through the adventures and dangers surrounding pivotal moments in Chicago history.

Historical, paperback, 352 pages, 5.1875" x 8"

Heartsong

Presents

Great Inspirational Romance at a Great Price!

Heartsong Presents books are inspirational romances in contemporary and historical settings, designed to give you an enjoyable, spirit-lifting reading experience. You can choose wonderfully written titles from some of today's best authors like Wanda E. Brunstetter, Mary Connealy, Susan Page Davis, Cathy Marie Hake, Joyce Livingston, and many others.

When ordering quantities less than six, above titles are $3.99 each.
Not all titles may be available at time of order.